SUGAR COOKIE COUNTRY HOUSE

HE FALLS FIRST SPORTS ROMANCE (SWEET & CLEAN)

HOCKEY SWEETHEARTS
BOOK SIX

JEAN ORAM

Sugar Cookie Country House
He Falls First Sports Romance (Sweet & Clean)

A Hockey Sweethearts Novel
By Jean Oram

© 2023 Jean Oram
All rights reserved, First Edition

Front cover design by Jess Mastorakos

Complete cataloguing information available online or upon request.

Oram, Jean.

Sugar Cookie Country House: He Falls First Sports Romance (Sweet & Clean) / Jean Oram.—1st. ed.

ISBN: 978-1-990833-68-7, 978-1-990833-69-4, 978-1-990833-70-0 (paperback), 978-1-990833-71-7, 978-1-990833-94-6 (large print), 978-1-989359-71-6 (ebook).

Oram Productions First Edition: April 2025

To my dog Fish.

You can thank my Jeansters for insisting I put you in this story. You didn't quite make the cut for the cover due to your big, black build. (I just couldn't quite make you work without making you look like a blob.) However, your personality and shenanigans—Houdini!— made it into the book. Too bad you can't read.

P.S. For readers who like games, be sure to check out "Find Fish" in the alternate, game version of the Sugar Cookie Country House's cover at www.jeanoram.com/Fish. See if you can find all nine of her in this fun version of the book's cover!

Sugar
Cookie
Country
House

Sugar Cookie Quilt House

CHAPTER 1

He was in love.

Dylan O'Neill had never met a woman like Jenny Oliver. She was curvy, had a generous smile and flashing blue-green eyes, a quick wit, bouncy chestnut hair and absolutely no qualms about knocking him down a peg.

The fact that he was a center for the San Antonio Dragons NHL team didn't matter to her. Neither did the paycheck nor the fame. She was the kind of woman who'd never allow the fact that he was a sought-after hockey player go to her head.

His parents had always claimed they'd fallen in love at first sight. Dylan had thought they were exaggerating, but now he could feel its possibility. There was something about Jenny that made him want to shush everyone at the packed Thanksgiving table and steer all conversation toward her.

By the time pie and cupcakes were set out, even though three of the eight guests were professional hockey players on strict no-dessert diets, the table had grown loud with chatter and laughter.

"Want one?" Dylan passed the plate of cupcakes to Jenny, seated to his left.

Her eyes lit up and she snagged one of the pale pink and yellow cupcakes, taking a big bite of the swirled frosting, her lashes drifting down in what was obviously pure pleasure.

"You make me miss sugar," he murmured, watching her eat.

"Life's too short, Dylan." She redirected the treats his way.

"Athena would kill me," he said, referring to the team's dietician who kept the players on a strict dietary leash.

Jenny nodded thoughtfully. "She totally would."

"You know her?"

"We went to school together. In second grade, she used to patrol the aisles and make sure we'd all eaten our carrot sticks before our cookies. She wasn't very popular, but the teacher loved her."

Dylan tried to imagine the commanding dietician with the olive skin behaving like that. "She does run a tight ship."

Jenny polished off her cupcake and he leaned closer, longing to wipe the bit of yellow frosting at the edge of her lush mouth. "You have something right there." He dabbed his own mouth, wishing it was hers.

Her shoulder brushed his as she quickly cleaned the spot with a napkin. "Thanks. Did I get it all?"

Her big eyes, a clear blue-green, stared up at him.

"Yeah." He tried to think of a way to keep their conversation going. "You watch hockey?"

"I'm more of a football gal. We all are around here. Go Torpedoes!"

The women at the table, all living in the small town of Sweetheart Creek, echoed her cheer.

"Who are the Torpedoes?" Dylan asked quietly.

"The high school team, silly. State champs." She gave his arm a gentle push, making him feel accepted despite his lack of local knowledge. He wondered what he needed to do to get her to do it again.

"I don't watch football," he admitted. He lived and breathed hockey. And when he wanted a change, he tended to choose basketball or NASCAR.

"For real? No football?"

"Too many players on the field." It was easy to miss a good setup happening elsewhere in the game when you were keeping your eye on the ball. It drove him nuts.

Jenny laughed and he felt the glow of her warmth. Whatever her life was like, it was clear that it was well-rounded and well-grounded, and also filled with many great things. Her constant happiness was evident in the smile lines forming around her mouth, the way her eyes sparkled and her laughter easily spilled from her. Was there a chance nobody had scooped her up yet? Could she be single?

"What?" Jenny's pale complexion grew redder and he realized he was staring.

"Nothing." Dylan quickly looked away, spotting the team's captain—the night's host—Maverick Blades, trying to swipe the second-last cupcake. Dylan was on his feet in a flash, despite the air cast on his right foot, and with a long-armed reach, snagged it from the man.

"You don't get dessert on your plan, old man," he said to Maverick. None of them, no matter their age, did during the playing season.

Maverick gave him a startled look and his girlfriend seated beside him, the former beauty queen Daisy-Mae Ray, started laughing.

"You're almost as old as I am!" Maverick told Dylan, face

flushed. He tried to snatch the dessert, but Dylan licked the swirled icing, claiming it. One of the things he loved most about being a Dragon were all of the shenanigans they pulled. Everyone on the team was quick to instigate mischief.

"You're both too old to have dessert," Leo, the team's newest right wing, called out.

Dylan and Maverick, both over the age of thirty and close to aging out of the National Hockey League, immediately teamed up, turning to face the rookie with stern glares.

"Excuse me?" Dylan asked Leo. He darted a quick look at Jenny who'd been giggling up to this point. Now she was silent, her eyes opened wide. He shot her a surreptitious wink to let her in on the joke, and she bit her bottom lip, her cheeks flushing pink.

Meanwhile, Leo was panicking, his fingers clutching the edge of the antique wood table, ready to flee.

"What was that, *Socks*?" Maverick asked, lowering his voice as he used Leo's dreaded team nickname.

"You calling us old?" Dylan chimed in.

"Just sayin'..." Leo edged his chair away from the table. "You know...with your broken foot and all... Rehab might be lengthy at your age and you might not—"

Dylan sucked in a steadying breath, his joking mood eroding with the truth of Leo's words. He made a quick motion with his good foot, as though he was going to lunge at the man. Leo moved so quickly, his chair tipped back, hitting the floor.

Everyone laughed and Dylan masked his limp as he returned to his seat, his foot screaming at him for being so stupid. But even worse was the fact that Leo was right.

Dylan knew what happened to players over the age of thirty. He knew what happened to players who got injured this late in their career. It could all be over and he just didn't know it yet. He took a mad bite of his cupcake, even though it was against dietary rules.

It could all be gone: the game, the camaraderie with his teammates, the sense of community and purpose. It might vanish in a flash if his broken foot decided it didn't want to mend itself back together as strong and good as it once was. And the ice time he was missing, as well as the games and intensive training? It wasn't great. All of it combined could prove to be the final nail in his career's coffin despite the trade talks centered on reuniting the fabled Double D—himself and his former Denver, Colorado teammate Darian Xavier. Everything hinged on his aching foot.

The table's conversation swirled around him as he focused on the throbbing at the top of his arch, and the fact that he'd eaten the entire forbidden cupcake in three giant bites.

"You okay?" Jenny asked, her eyes a darker color, as if they served as a mood ring. Current mood: worried.

"Tell me what you do." Realizing his tone was sharp, he softened it. "Daisy-Mae said you have a store in town?"

Her smile flashed quick and bright. "I have a western wear boutique called Blue Tumbleweed on Main Street." She gestured in the direction of the small town, located a few miles from Maverick's ranch. Her eyes danced over Dylan's dress pants and white shirt. "If you're going to hang around Sweetheart Creek, you're going to need some jeans. Pop in and I'll suit you up so you fit in."

"Who says I want to?" He hadn't fit in anywhere—other than with his hockey pals—so why try now?

"You don't want to look like a cowboy?"

He shook his head. Despite living on a dairy farm as a teen, a cowboy hat, boots, and tight jeans were not his thing.

"You're not a small town guy?" Jenny's head tipped to the side, as if trying to figure him out.

He opened his mouth to reply, realizing he wasn't actually sure *what* he was anymore. He'd grown up in the Netherlands with an Irish father, then moved to California where surfing was popular—although he'd never tried it—then had spent time on a Wisconsin dairy farm before leaving it all to live in cities and play hockey for a living. Outside of hockey, who was he? Where was *home*?

"Well," she said, a hint of Texas drawl coming out as her hand rested briefly on his forearm and leaving a trail of heat that expanded up past his elbow. "We can make you into a small town fella if it pleases you."

His eyes met the kindness in hers, and he couldn't think of anything he'd like more than to fit into her world.

* * *

An hour ago, Jenny had arrived at Maverick's for the post-Thanksgiving celebration—arranged as close to the holiday as the players' schedules allowed—feeling wiped. It was Black Friday, the beginning of her multi-day sale, and her store had been chaos from opening to closing. Tomorrow she'd have to go in early, reconcile her cash register's receipts and refold an endless amount of clothing that had been pulled from stacks by eager customers, not to mention reorganize the racks of shirts and jeans that had once been meticulously sorted by size. But right now, all she wanted was to lock up, walk away and never come back.

Maybe she'd even march right out of Sweetheart Creek and the life that had become somewhat predictable and boring.

Except who would have predicted that she'd sit beside a hockey player at dinner, an NHLer who was cute, gruff, but also sweet and so down to earth it made her soul dance. She'd been thinking that a bit of travel might revive her and pull her out of the small town doldrums. After all, who wanted to see the rest of their lives unspooling in front of them in a straight line of repetition? But that was what her future was looking like...and it sure didn't give her thrills of anticipation. She hadn't ever expected to be sandwiched between two pro hockey players at Thanksgiving. And she especially hadn't foreseen that one of them would flirt with her with a telltale twinkle in his eyes, as if they were sharing some secret joke.

She glanced toward her blond friend, Daisy-Mae, wondering if the woman was trying to set her up with Dylan. Sort of a ridiculous thought, to be honest. But Jenny had been set up enough times in her thirty-one years to do the math. Going around the table, it was clear she and Dylan were the odd ones out. She mentally noted the couples. There were Maverick and Daisy-Mae. Dak, the retired player to her left, was involved with the team's owner, Miranda Fairchild. Then across from Jenny was her friend Violet, the team's mascot, who obviously only had eyes for the former rodeo king and current NHL rookie, Leo. That left three obvious singles: Maverick's mom, who was in charge of the meal, herself, and Dylan. Maybe she and Dylan were just here to fill all the seats at the table?

Because how could Daisy-Mae see anything working out relationship-wise between Jenny and a man who lived over an hour away and could get traded at pretty much any time of the year? And anyway, Jenny must seem horribly small town and boring to a man like Dylan. Sure, she had a great life. Really great, actually, and with nothing to truly complain about. But she instinctively knew she wasn't his type. She was not at all glamorous, a bit too curvy to be fashionable, and, according to her grandfather, too bossy for her own good. Probably because she'd become the self-appointed boss of him after he broke his hip two years ago.

Dylan gently elbowed Jenny, his arm softly bumping hers. He lifted his chin toward the platter of turkey, one of his mussy locks of sandy hair falling across his forehead.

"Say please," she chided playfully.

His eyes locked on hers, gray and filled with secrets she longed to uncover. "*Please.*"

She suppressed an anticipatory shiver as his deep voice rumbled through her and passed the turkey, refusing to release it until he muttered what sounded like an amused 'thank you.'

Carol, Maverick's mom, turned to her. "Are you two dating?"

"Sure," Jenny said lightly, "I'm his girlfriend."

Dylan's retort was quick. "I'm going to hold you to that."

There was a seriousness in his tone that straightened her spine. She turned to face him better, aware the table had gone silent.

"I'd like to see you try," she said evenly, squelching the thrill that was hammering at her mental restraint, trying to break it down.

She'd been love-bombed and charmed by Ranger Torrington a few years back and had learned her lesson—that sweet words weren't always backed with true intent. She wasn't about to be made a fool of again—especially by someone who lived along the edges of the limelight, and who could accidentally make that humiliation very, very public.

"I always need someone to be my plus one."

Yeah, right. She could just see herself on his arm at fancy hockey events, such as next month's black tie gala for the Dragons' Charity for Sick Kids. She shook her head. Dylan was truly taking the flirting too far. The man probably had a virtual little black book thicker than the tattered old Yellow Pages her grandfather kept kicking around to use as a step stool in his clothes closet. As fun as the flirting was, it might be time to end this before things got out of hand and she started to think this was more real than it was.

"Are you asking me if I'm interested?" she asked carefully.

"I don't know. Are you?" His gaze was serious, as if trying to gauge her interest.

"Do you make the woman foot the bill?"

He looked offended, his shoulders going back against his chair.

"How about holding doors? Would you do that?" Jenny narrowed her eyes, eager to see if Dylan would pick up on the fact that she was not looking for an old-fashioned boyfriend. She was thirty-one and used to doing things on her own.

"Depends," Dylan replied slowly. "Do you like that? Or do you find it annoying?"

"Annoying," she admitted, sitting back in her chair, watching him, curious as to why he seemed so serious about feeling out her potential as a future date.

Could it be that he was genuinely interested, despite how her friend had obviously thrown them together?

"Good. Then I won't." His gray eyes softened. "Unless you're wearing an impossible dress and need help to get out of the car." His gaze lingered on her curves.

She scoffed, feeling suddenly warm. "Do I look like I wear impossible dresses?" She'd practically been born wearing jeans.

"You own a clothing store. You might."

"And you drive a car?" she asked. "Not a truck?"

"I do. Problem with that?" She could feel him mentally crossing his arms. He seemed to be loving her pushback as much as she was enjoying dishing it out.

"I don't know. Do you have a problem with the fact that *I* drive a truck?" She batted her lashes at him and she saw the flicker of a hidden grin play at the edges of his mouth.

"Not at all. My masculinity is safe and sound."

Her eyes drifted to his wide, strong shoulders, the flatness of his chest, the bulge of his biceps under his crisp shirt. Yes, he had masculinity locked up all right.

Her voice was embarrassingly breathy as she murmured, "Good to hear."

He leaned an elbow on the table, shifting so his body was square to her. He dropped his voice low as though trying to act seductive, but she saw it for what it was—his own test—as he asked, "Do you go ga-ga for hockey stars?"

Instinctively, she knew he wouldn't like that, to be treated differently because of his profession. The fame, from what she'd noted tonight, hadn't gotten to him. She'd met the odd NHLer such as Mullens, the team's popular forward, who seemed a bit full of himself in a strangely charming way, but otherwise, most of the other players were surprisingly real. So real that the hockey millionaires spent most of their rare days off here, in Maverick's eighty-year-old farmhouse, helping him renovate its wiring, plumbing and who knew what else.

In the split second she considered how to answer, Leo made a lame joke about Dylan's injury and how he was hardly a player, let alone a star. Dylan ignored the man, keeping his focus on Jenny, a muscle in his jaw flexing. She had a fleeting curiosity about what a broken foot might mean to his career.

But back to his question. No, she'd never go ga-ga. It wasn't her style. But if she did end up going somewhere as his plus-one, would she be cool with the attention he'd draw? Would she act crazy and embarrass him? Or would she keep calm and help him, the way Daisy-Mae was helping Maverick transform his tarnished image? She understood that being a hockey star put you in the public eye, and that the results were not always positive. But what would it truly be like in Dylan's shoes or in the shoes beside him?

She gave a shrug, deciding to be bluntly honest. "I could take a star or leave him." She propped an elbow on the table, echoing Dylan's posture, her tone sweet. "Do you have a problem with a woman owning her own business, and sometimes being too busy to fawn all over your stardom?"

"Sometimes." Dylan's smile was quick and sincere.

Well, there was her answer. He might seem down to earth, but he wanted a fangirl for a girlfriend. Yuck.

Jenny sat back, thanking Carol for the meal, knowing that even though Maverick was technically their host, his mom had been the one to make it all happen.

"I like having my girlfriend around," Dylan grumbled to her, his tone frustrated as though he'd figured out she hadn't liked his answer. "What's the point of a relationship if you don't want to spend time with the woman you've chosen? It's not about stardom. It's about *time*."

He tapped the table with a hand to emphasize his next words. "Making time."

Jenny eyed him, noting his earnestness and need to be understood. She'd assumed his off-putting confession had come from a place of ego, but maybe it had actually come from somewhere sweet. She appreciated how genuine and honest he was about what he wanted in a relationship, even if his way of expressing it had been a bit awkward.

Everyone at the table shifted with discomfort, as though they'd witnessed a couple fighting. But Jenny understood Dylan and where he was coming from.

"You own a store," he went on, his tone slightly more gruff, a hint of a Dutch accent appearing. "I'm sure you get it. You have busy times just like I do. But if you love someone and they're important to you, you find the time. You *always* find the time."

She let his sentiments sink in, thinking about her grandfather, the reason she hadn't sold her store and flown off to explore and discover adventure. Years ago, he'd fallen while getting out of his armchair after his leg had gone to sleep. Out of reach of the phone, he'd lain on the floor in pain with his broken hip for almost a full day before she'd stopped by and found him.

With the lease on the place she'd been renting about to expire, Jenny had moved in with him, helping him with his rehab and daily living. He was better now, but with no other family regularly in town, she'd stayed on because he was important to her. And even with running her store, she found the time to be with him, to bring him lunch in the middle of her day, to drive him out to one of her brother's places outside the city of San Antonio so he could spend this long weekend with them while she worked.

She turned to Dylan, feeling his words in her heart. "You're right. It is important. Really important."

But unfortunately, even though she was open to the idea of falling in love with an exciting man like Dylan, she just couldn't see how their two lives would ever mesh in a way that would give them that expanse of time together that they both seemed to crave.

CHAPTER 2

$\mathcal{J}$enny Oliver was going to stop thinking about Dylan O'Neill. Today. She was going to erase him and his dancing, storm-cloud eyes from her mind, along with the endless fantasy-riddled 'what-ifs' centered on the possibility of him asking her out on a date.

Just because their flirting had been the most fun she'd had in ages, and he made her feel all fizzy inside as well as seen by him, it didn't mean he wanted to start something between them. Honestly, she needed to get a grip because, seriously. An NHL player? The man's life was the complete opposite of hers. Always on the road, aware he could move to new cities and teams at any time, living in a tax bracket she'd never-ever see… She very much doubted he would ever fall for her, give up hockey, and then settle down in her hometown of Sweetheart Creek, Texas, population 4,123. Or keep playing hockey and ask her to tag along.

Although that would be pretty exciting.

She steered her pickup truck down a gravel road outside of town, her thoughts of Dylan refusing to be shed as she drove closer to the home where they'd first met. Just thinking about him and that Thanksgiving dinner got her all stirred up and her pulse racing. She slowly exhaled, steadying herself. Daisy-Mae had admitted to giving him Jenny's number after she'd gone home that night. That had been five days ago. Shouldn't he have called or texted if he was interested?

She shook her head. It was time she read the signs and shifted her fantasies back to what it might be like to travel to Spain or to take a cruise when she had a bit more freedom.

As she took in the vehicles parked in front of Maverick's, she climbed from her truck, suddenly overcome by jitters. She'd heard it was renovation day at Maverick's again and had decided it would be a good time to pick up the salad bowl she'd left behind last Friday.

Not because Dylan might be here.

Her cowboy boots hit the dry dirt along the edge of the driveway, sending up puffs of dust as a hawk circled the barn out back. As the sound of a power saw filled the air, she caught herself scouring the parked cars, on the lookout for one that could be Dylan's. Even though his foot was currently in a plastic Velcroed boot, it sounded like he was a regular on Mav's crew.

Let's see. The Mustang was Maverick's. The shiny black SUV would belong to single dad Landon. The truck was former rodeo star Leo's. Dylan had said he drove a car. Was the Caddy his? She snorted in amusement at the unorthodox choice as she made her way to the faded old house that had seen better days.

The home's front steps creaked and at the door, Jenny straightened her new, deep pink checkered blouse and dusted the thighs of her new jeans. The fresh outfit wasn't in case she saw Dylan. No, it was simply because after going back to her natural brown hair color, all of her clothes seemed boring. At least, that was what she told herself. And anyway, what was the point of owning your own boutique if you didn't sometimes use it as your personal closet? And the cute beaded necklace? That was just an extra treat for the long hours she'd put in during her Black Friday sale.

Jenny knocked on the screen door's frame, the sound of a power saw and male voices continuing to drift through the opening.

"Hello?" she called, pulling on the door's handle. The whole frame suddenly swung downward as the top hinges came free from the rotten door frame. She let out an involuntary squawk and flailed her free hand to protect herself.

An arm reached past her, righting the door. The arm smelled like the outdoors and fresh nail polish.

"Thank you," she said, looking up before doing a double take at the man standing at her side.

It was Dylan O'Neill. But his mussed up shaggy locks were pulled back by a sparkly plastic tiara and smeared across his scowling lips was bright pink lipstick. He looked like he'd passed out drunk and been pranked by buddies. Or been playing tea party with Landon Jackson's four-year-old daughter.

Dylan's strong hands held the door upright, protecting her from being bludgeoned while she stared at him in stupefied shock.

His voice was an even deeper timbre than she'd remembered as he said, "Hi."

She found the ability to speak after several attempts. "Right. Hi."

She blinked at him, unmoving, her eyes following his muscular, corded arms to the door, noting that his fingernails were a sparkly rainbow of messy colors. Her heart hiccupped at the idea that Dylan had a secret, tender side where he was great with kids.

With a sinking heart she realized that distracting herself with thoughts of cruises and foreign trips was never going to work when it came to Dylan O'Neill, because now, there was no way she was ever going to be able to forget him.

* * *

With a quick yank, Dylan removed the screen door from the frame like it had only been held there by tape. He leaned it against the house's yellow outer wall. Maverick's place would probably be better served by being bulldozed, but the man seemed more than happy to pour money into it while he hid from the world. And with the media storm villainizing him in rumors concerning him and the wife of the owner of his former team in Lafayette, Dylan honestly couldn't blame him. And because he was helping out Mav, Dylan could allow himself to be distracted from worrying about his foot and the long-term impact the injury might have on his career.

And speaking of distractions, he was currently staring at the pretty cowgirl who'd captured his interest at Thanksgiving dinner. He'd believed his imagination had blown her prettiness out of proportion, but when she gave him one of those sunny smiles that blasted him with warmth, he knew his memory hadn't tricked him.

"I like the new look," Jenny said, her tone sassy as she brushed past him into the home's entry. Her eyes flashed over him, carrying a hint of amusement.

Right. The lipstick and nail polish. It wasn't exactly how

he'd imagined being dressed while he'd been rehearsing ways to convince her to come out on a date with him.

"I'm babysitting," he grumbled as an explanation.

"It's not babysitting if I'm here!" called a voice from inside the house. Landon Jackson; four-year-old Rylnn's dad. With Dylan sidelined from some of the renovation work due to his injury, he and Rylnn had become pals. The kid was a hoot, but at the moment he was really regretting letting her do the tea party dress-up thing on him today. He supposed he should be grateful she hadn't forced him into a dress.

Jenny's gaze settled over his jeans and faded concert T-shirt as though reading his mind. She tsked. Remembering the plastic tiara perched in his hair, he snatched it and cleared his throat, wishing he had something witty to say.

"I pegged your makeover style all wrong." Jenny's eyes danced as she looked up, her gaze trailing lazily over his torso and shoulders as though enjoying the results of his grueling dry-land training. "You were right. The cowboy look would be all wrong. This is much more you. But you should still come by the Blue Tumbleweed to complete your makeover. I have a lovely wraparound dress that might suit you."

"Ha. Ha," he said dryly. "I was going to ask you out, but now I think I've changed my mind."

Her jaw dropped, and she looked as disappointed as Rylnn had when he'd told her there'd be no glitter earlier today. The stuff got everywhere. He glanced down, noting that despite his ban, his cast was still somehow peppered with pink and purple sparkles. He leaned his head back in despair. "Oh, come on!"

"What?" Jenny asked in alarm.

"Nothing," he said quickly. "Rylnn!" he called into the adjoined living room, summoning the small girl.

Rylnn came bouncing to the entry, her wild black curls waving, a melting popsicle dripping down her hand, her chin already an orange mess. Without thinking, Dylan swiped at the drips with the hem of his shirt before they landed on her flouncy princess dress and instigated a national crisis. The girl loved that outfit more than life itself.

"We had a glitter deal, kiddo, and you broke it."

"I want my tiara back," Rylnn said, snagging it from his grip. Then she scowled back at him, imitating his look while she plunked the extra tiara on her head so she was now wearing two. Defiant and adorable. How did Landon ever find it in his heart to discipline this kid? He must have to look the other way when he told her 'no' to something.

"Lovin' the boots," Jenny drawled, crouching to be at Rylnn's eye level.

The girl grinned and did a twirl, then stuck out one small cowboy boot, then the other for Jenny's inspection.

"Very nice," she said with approval.

"I'm a cowgirl princess," Rylnn announced.

"She's my best customer," Jenny told Dylan, gesturing to Rylnn as she straightened up again.

It didn't surprise him. He'd yet to meet anyone who could say no to the little charmer.

He pointed to his right foot, encased in a hard plastic mold, black padding and Velcro. "What am I supposed to do with this, Ry? Buy a new one? It's impossible to get glitter out of Velcro."

Rylnn gave an unbothered shrug. "It's okay. You're rich."

Beside him, Jenny giggled, and his stern act melted a bit further.

"It's just glitter," Jenny said nonchalantly, her tone hinting that she was very aware of just how often he would get teased for showing up at the rink with sparkles stuck to his injured foot.

"I'll lose my man card," he muttered, shaking his head.

"Bye," Rylnn chirped, zipping back into the construction zone. He should follow her, make sure someone had eyes on her.

"She's cute," Jenny said.

"Freaking adorable. She's the worst."

"What?" Jenny laughed. She was eyeing him as though trying to figure him out.

He shook his head. He couldn't explain the way the little girl had twisted his heart in her small fist, fully owning it. When he had kids, he was going to be doomed.

Jenny frowned at him, then took two steps back, disappearing into the powder room off the entry. She appeared a second later, a wad of toilet paper wrapped around her hand. Before he could react, she had his chin in a firm grip and was wiping his mouth.

He tried to pull back, but she held him in place, her touch becoming more tender when he stopped fighting. He'd noticed her mood ring eyes at Thanksgiving, but he hadn't seen this softer blue-green tone. She smelled different today, too. Less like that strange new clothing scent—as if she'd been sleeping in a pile of new blue jeans—and more like baked apples and cinnamon.

"There." She released him and stood back. "Back to being a handsome stud."

"Hey, who's here?" Maverick appeared in the small entry, frowning at his now-absent screen door as a skinny cat came waltzing in as though she owned the place. He gave Jenny a funny look. "Did you literally break down my door to come and fight with this guy again?"

Jenny turned to Dylan, that big sunshine smile widening her mouth. "Sure did! But he says he doesn't want me so I guess that's the end of that." She gave a fake pout that made him long to pull her into his arms and show her just how wrong that claim was.

"Beggars can't be choosers, Dylan," Maverick muttered. "Nobody's lining up to date your grumpy butt. Although truthfully, Jenny's way out of your league."

Dylan darted a glare at Maverick, and Jenny shot Dylan a smug, satisfied smile that made her eyes sparkle.

She turned to Maverick. "Actually, I came for my salad bowl. I left it here on Friday."

"I'll go grab it. Wait here. The place is a disaster again," he said, a loud power-saw punctuating his statement.

"So you didn't come here to see me?" Dylan asked Jenny, noting her cheeks turned pinker than they'd already been.

She laughed. "I came to get the last word in that fight everyone thinks we had."

"Were we fighting?" he asked, genuinely curious if he'd misread the whole night. Maverick had hinted several times that he'd been a grumpy jerk. He'd even gone so far as to say that he had no game off the ice. "I thought we were..." He paused, as though searching for the right term.

"Flirting?"

"Yeah." Definitely flirting.

Jenny was a sweet, small town woman and he didn't want to scare her off by coming on to her too aggressively. He'd learned that the busy, high-profile life he'd acclimatized to over time—and now took for granted—sometimes freaked people out. He wanted to get to know her, convince her they might have something special flaring between them without something in his world spooking her. Because when it came right down to it, he was just a regular guy who was looking for a life with friends and laughter, a woman who loved him and, eventually, a family.

"Well, whatever it was, it was fun," she said, her eyes fluttering away from his as though shy. "I rarely push back against people like that." Her gaze met his. "At least without them running for the hills."

"Push as much as you want."

She laughed nervously.

"You're strong," he said, brushing a strand of hair off her face.

"Yeah?" she asked, her voice soft with invitation to say more.

"And you need someone strong in return. Someone who can take a challenge and dish it back." *Me.*

She'd edged closer. Or maybe he had.

"Is that what I need?" Her eyes were on his mouth and he realized he was cupping her elbow, leaning in. He straightened, very aware that he wanted to get this right, and that meant not rushing into a kiss, no matter how much he desired one. If he seemed as though he was playing her in any way, she'd be long gone.

"I was going to call you," Dylan admitted, his voice low, as if it was just the two of them, and the small house wasn't teeming with hockey players and their power tools.

"Why didn't you?"

"I have no clue." And he didn't. He had a million excuses, from his schedule, to a fear that he'd misread the situation like Maverick had implied. But none of them were good enough reasons as to why he hadn't picked up his phone to call this sweet woman and say hi.

Maverick called out, "Found it!" his feet thumping across the hardwood floors.

Seconds later, Jenny hesitated in the doorway with her wooden bowl. She said quietly, "Call me if you want to, okay?"

* * *

Jenny, halfway to her red truck, pulled her ringing phone from her back pocket. Unknown number. Figuring it could be a supplier for her store, she answered, the late November wind toying with her hair.

"Hey, it's Dylan."

A smile stretched across Jenny's face and she convinced herself not to turn around to see if Dylan was standing in Maverick's doorway, watching her.

"Oh, hey. Long time no see. How's the foot treating you?"

He chuckled, the sound low and welcoming. "It could heal faster."

"So what's up?" She climbed into her truck, handing the call off to the vehicle's system so it came through the speakers.

Dylan was intriguing and quiet, and she liked him. But their established lives were located over an hour away from each other and they lived in very different worlds. A man like him would probably never amount to anything more than an adventure.

She glanced toward the aged farmhouse. Still, she wanted adventure. Badly.

"Did you forget to kiss me goodbye?" she teased, her skin heating at what had felt like an almost-kiss just moments earlier. She'd been sure it was going to happen. His words about her being strong and needing someone who could dish it back had made her head feel all swirly, as if he was offering to be that person.

"I did," he said, his voice smooth velvet. "I also didn't ask you out."

She held her breath, glad he couldn't see her in the truck, grinning foolishly.

"Oh?" she asked, toying with her necklace. "Do you need me to run back in, or shall we leave it until next time?"

"Next time," he said firmly, leaving no doubt in her mind that Dylan O'Neill had had plans to ask her out…and to kiss her. The sound of power tools in the call's background suddenly grew quieter, and she wondered if he'd stepped out back or into a room. She could hear him mutter something to Rylnn. "Sorry," he said into the phone. "You around later in the week?"

"So soon? Afraid I'll forget you?"

"Afraid someone else will scoop you up."

Her heart lifted and soared. She could pretty much guarantee nobody'd find her in Sweetheart Creek. Almost everyone her age was either married, on their way to it, or she'd already dated them.

"Well," she said carefully, "that could happen. Best to be cautious. What are you thinking?"

"Do you like McKenzie's?"

"McKenzie's?" She nearly choked. The fanciest restaurant in San Antonio? She wasn't even sure she had the right kind of outfit to dine in a place so upscale—despite having unrestricted access to a fully-stocked clothing store. "Well, hon, I'll let you in on a secret. If I can't wear my boots, I'm not all that interested."

His tone was amused as he suggested another place she'd

never heard of. "Landon and Leo claim it has the best TexMex in the state."

"Hm." She pretended to consider the offer, knowing she'd go anywhere with him, even McKenzie's. "What about a barn dance?"

"I'd rather be shot than listen to country music all night."

She sputtered over the bluntness of his statement. "Well, then."

"You like country music, don't you?" he asked, his voice low with what she hoped wasn't dejection.

"I do."

"How about I come into town sometime and we'll figure out what to do?"

Her heart sank as she put the truck in gear, steering it down Maverick's driveway and back toward Sweetheart Creek. "Sure," she said lightly, betraying her plummeting spirits, knowing that she'd blown her one shot. "Sounds like a plan."

CHAPTER 3

*D*ylan should never be allowed to talk to women over the phone. He felt like he'd blown it with Jenny last Wednesday. It had started off great in Maverick's hallway, both of them flirting and almost kissing. Then he'd called her, thinking he was being charming. The flirting had continued, and then boom! He'd crashed and burned. No survivors—he'd heard it in her voice, the richness of her tone flattening.

Well, he wanted a second shot and he wasn't leaving anything to chance by picking up the phone again. So he was here, in Sweetheart Creek, to ask her out.

She liked country music and barn dances—two things he was not a fan of. And yet, the woman and her differences had somehow made his attraction even stronger. Maybe it was because she said what she thought and felt with no regard to whether it would make him like her or not. She was just *her*. And after being in the limelight for so many years and being treated as if he was a god who couldn't handle people's truest feelings, her genuineness was refreshing. Intoxicating like a lungful of fresh air after being under water for too long.

"Do you go ga-ga for hockey stars?"

"I could take them or leave them."

He'd fallen for her right then and there at the Thanksgiving table.

And he was determined to make this work.

He parked his car on Main Street and stopped beneath the boutique's navy and white Blue Tumbleweed sign. The store's front window was decorated with fake snow and a Christmas tree. Mannequins wearing mostly green and red western wear showed off the latest fashions for both men and women.

Two cowgirls stood by the window, pointing to a handwritten New Arrivals banner. The taller, slender woman pointed to a pair of pink boots that didn't fit the holiday theme, and made him think of Landon's daughter Rylnn.

The woman said, "Could you imagine the look on Levi's face if I wore those into the riding ring?"

The woman beside her laughed, sending her feather earrings swinging. "I'll buy you the boots if you let me be there to see it."

The two leaned into each other as they laughed, walking into the diner next door, a bell tinkling to announce their arrival.

Small towns. He missed them. The connections and inside jokes based on a shared history, and the sense of belonging. He hadn't truly had those in a deep or long-term kind of way growing up, but what little he'd experienced had been good.

They were also the things he'd miss if he left hockey.

Dylan pushed his hands deeper into the pockets of his jeans, hunching further into his suit jacket as the evening breeze whispered past. The air smelled like rain and for a moment, he wished he was back in Wisconsin, where it had already snowed. That, to him, was Christmas. Not rain. Not the odd garden still pushing out winter vegetables like they were in this part of Texas.

Dylan opened the door to Jenny's shop and was hit with a blast of Christmas country music playing from a nearby speaker.

He sighed, wondering if he was wasting his time pursuing a cowgirl whose interests were so different from his own.

"Howdy," a woman said from behind a rack of jeans, ignoring the banging that was coming from a back room that was sectioned off by a sheet of plastic. She had curves like Jenny, although hers were enhanced by a pregnancy. Her shoulder-length brown hair looked as if she'd cut it herself and she set down a steaming cup of tea that smelled of apples and cinnamon. "I'm April. Can I help you find something?"

Where was Jenny? It hadn't even occurred to him she might not be here.

In his mind, he'd imagined that he'd simply arrive and ask her out. She'd say yes, then magically reappear in a dangerous dress, dipping low, hugging tightly around her middle and her curvy build. They'd eat, they'd laugh, and that was it. The beginning of them.

Only it wasn't looking like it would be that way at all.

* * *

"Sorry? What did you say?" Jenny looked up from her computer's keyboard where she was adding a collection of newly commissioned necklaces to the store's digitized inventory. She focused on her shop assistant and friend, April Wylder.

"I said, there's a hottie looking for you."

Jenny was already getting out of her chair before the word 'hottie' registered and she fell back into her seat.

"I think he's a Dragon," April whispered, even though there was no way the man could hear them through the office wall or the hammering that had started up in the store's construction zone. When the flirty, fun phone call between herself and Dylan had suddenly soured last Wednesday, it had brought her straight back down to earth. Itching for something to take her mind off of him, she'd jumped into the previously abandoned store expansion plan that would give her more space for displaying formal attire samples. She'd decided that if she couldn't find excitement with Dylan, then hey, maybe expanding the shop would pull her out of her life's current slump. Today, even though it was Saturday, was the first day of the planned month-long construction headache and she was already regretting her decision.

"It can't be Maverick again," Jenny mused aloud. "Unless he forgot something?" He'd been in that morning asking what Daisy-Mae might like for Christmas. He'd bought some choice items that would surely delight her friend.

"It's not Maverick," April confirmed. Since San Antonio had created their NHL expansion team, and some of the team's hockey players had discovered their small town and the few remaining single women within it, a few of Jenny's friends had become *very* interested in the sport. Even pregnant, happily married ones such as April. "This one says he's here to ask you out."

Jenny swiveled in her chair to face April more fully. "What? But he can't...we..." She frowned at April, who smiled and shrugged.

"Maybe the call didn't go as bad as you thought," her friend said, rubbing her growing belly.

April had heard all about the recent exchange when Jenny had come slamming back into the store, muttering loudly about men—and Dylan in particular—then right back out again when she realized she'd forgotten to take lunch to her grandfather.

"He hates country music," Jenny said pointedly, as though this was key evidence in the case against Dylan and why something would never work out between them.

"A lot of people do."

"He must be bored." He'd probably decided that while he was injured, he might as well find a girlfriend to keep him occupied. Unable to resist, Jenny had read up on him a bit, surprised to learn he was a coveted player in the midst of trade talks despite his injury. From what she'd gathered, he played well with some Darian guy and they'd been nicknamed Double D due to the fact that their names both started with Ds. Honestly, it was a dumb name. Neither of them played defense, which was often shortened to 'D.' Sports and the sports world was weirder than she'd realized.

"Hm. Who else around here is bored?" April asked, feigning thoughtfulness.

Her poor friend had already heard Jenny's 'is this all there is for me?' moanings and groanings more than once over the past several months.

Jenny rolled her eyes and stood up. "As soon as his foot heals, he'll be out of here, mark my words."

"So what? Not everything has to lead to a wedding. Go have some fun and let this prego with the swollen ankles live vicariously through you." April pushed Jenny toward the door that led into the store.

"I don't kiss and tell."

"Oooh. Kissing. There's nothing like a first kiss. I bet he's amazing. He's got that moody, determined vibe going on. Kind of sexy, if you ask me. Sometimes Brant is just so... sweet. Too sweet. You know?"

Jenny scooted forward and clapped her hands over her ears in case her friend got into details about her and her husband's love life. April's hormones were all over the place with her pregnancy, and it wasn't uncommon for Jenny to be on the receiving end of TMI.

"For the record, grumpy men should not be considered sexy!" she said before fleeing to the front. She brushed past a rack of sample wedding dresses sporting a western flare, on loan from a local company. She slowed when she reached the cash register and smoothed out her green blouse with the pretty pink stitching over the pockets.

Sure enough, Dylan O'Neill was in the middle of her store wearing a pair of dark wash jeans—casual fit—a white dress shirt that looked like it had been tailored to fit his torso perfectly and a dark navy suit jacket over it. As always, his sandy hair needed a cut, the longish bits at his crown ruffled and adorable. She watched as he took in the shelves of jeans with his deep, broody eyes and a frown that seemed to be looking for an excuse to lift upward. Any time he sent her a hint of a smile, it felt like she'd reached the highest level in the Dylan puzzle, a level nobody else had ever reached.

Man, he was tweaking her sense of equilibrium. She felt lightheaded and way too warm looking at him. She wished she'd at least washed her hair that morning and put on a better bra. She needed to get with the program. Especially if hunky NHLers were moseying around, stopping by to ask her out.

No. Don't get your hopes up too high.

The man lived in a different universe and appeared to be her total opposite. Maybe he was actually here because he'd changed his mind about his style—although, truth be told, his tailored shirt and suit jacket were way sexier than anything she kept in stock. He might even be here to pick up another pair of cowboy boots for Rylnn in hopes of helping coax her out of the princess phase.

But what if April hadn't misunderstood him, and he really was here to ask Jenny out? What if he really did like how she unleashed her unfiltered thoughts and feelings around him? She hated to admit it, but nobody made her feel and act as free as Dylan O'Neill did.

"Hey, stranger," she said. "Heard you want a mulligan."

"What?" Dylan turned, his brow wrinkling in confusion.

"I thought hockey players golfed. A mulligan is a do-over."

"I know what it is. Why do I want one?"

"Because..." She shook her head, not wanting to get into the awkward and disappointing end to the last time they'd connected. With luck, this would be a fresh start. "April said you're here to ask me out?"

The frown vanished and she felt the reward of that special smile he shared here and there. "I am. Are you busy?"

"Right now?"

"Yes."

She gestured to the store. "I'm kind of working, Dylan." Was this what he'd hinted at over Thanksgiving, that he expected a woman to drop everything to spend time with him? Maybe he'd been more honest about the fawn-over-my-stardom thing than she'd realized.

He pushed up his jacket sleeve, checking his watch. "Store closes in five. Go for supper?"

"I still have things to do after I turn off the Open sign and lock the door."

"I'll wait." He started rearranging the stacks of jeans on the shelves along the back wall.

She cringed at the way he was pulling out pairs and putting them back in a different spot. She'd spent hours resorting the jeans after holding her three-day-long Black Friday sale. She stepped around a rack, reaching for a pair that looked about right. "What size do you want? This brand fits a little snug, but these should fit."

He placed a hand over hers, stopping her. The warmth of his grip traveled through her. His eyes met hers. "I don't want jeans."

"Oh." She put the denim back, her fingers trembling. "Well then, quit messing up my system."

He turned back to the shelves. "You don't want these organized by size?"

"I do." She looked at the shelf, sighing as she realized the last customer had caused a new mess.

Dylan was already resorting the piles for her.

"You don't have to do that," she said.

He shrugged. "May as well make myself useful while I wait."

Jenny blinked and turned to see if April was eavesdropping. She was. She lifted her hands in question and April said, her voice carrying, "How about you two run along? I can close up."

"Thanks." Dylan snagged Jenny's hand, pulling her toward the wide aisle that led to the front door. "Need your purse or anything?"

"Wow. Bossy much?" Jenny asked, slowing her steps, then breaking away to head into the back room to grab her things.

"I didn't even say yes, you know."

"We could tell you wanted to," April said from the doorway, grinning from ear to ear.

As Jenny grabbed her coat, she heard Dylan say to April, "I dated a semi-famous singer back in Denver and she never made me work this hard."

"I'm worth it," Jenny said, breezing past him, ready to go.

"You sure are," he said, moving ahead to hold the door for her.

As he watched her pass him, she had a feeling that she wouldn't be complaining about being bored for much longer.

CHAPTER 4

Jenny was gorgeous in tight jeans and a Western blouse—green today—her brown hair pulled into a perky ponytail. Her eyes sparkled and her expression was filled with such happy expectation as they walked the block and a half to the Watering Hole that Dylan almost looked behind him to see if someone else was following them.

She slipped her arm through his as they jaywalked across the street.

"I thought I'd chased you off forever," she admitted.

"I'm starting to think you're trying."

"Me? Chasing you off?" She blinked at him.

"I asked you out and you chose a tavern? Don't they play country music?"

She laughed. "Just like everywhere else in town. This is Texas, hon."

He shook his head. It was a shame she didn't have the time tonight to come into the city for a proper date. He'd have liked to take her to a nice restaurant in San Antonio. Afterwards, they could have strolled down the Riverwalk hand in hand, and he'd have made sure to give her a thorough good-night kiss. But she'd told him she had a grandfather at home waiting for his supper, as well as chickens to look after. So the best he'd get tonight was a quick plate of wings at the tavern. It wasn't exactly on his dietary plan—or his dream date—but he'd survive.

A few minutes later they were sipping their drinks—a peppermint hot chocolate for her, and decaf for him—and waiting on their wings.

"So?" Jenny leaned back with her cup of hot chocolate and Dylan echoed her posture, then swung his uninjured left foot up to rest on top of his right knee. The table was small, and the place fairly quiet for a Saturday evening. The walls were covered with flashing neon signs advertising beer brands, and in a raised area near the back, he saw pool tables. He was pretty sure the vibe of the tavern would change once the clock dialed past suppertime.

"So… This is an official date?" she asked.

"Yes."

As silence stretched between them, he fought the urge to explain that this one didn't truly count because it wasn't an accurate representation of what he thought a date should be.

"Do you still go to hockey games even though you can't play?" she asked.

He nodded.

"It must be fun playing a sport for a living."

He gave a sound of acknowledgement and she raised her brows, obviously expecting more of an answer.

"It's grueling."

He supposed he'd thought it was fun when he'd first started, and before he'd been injured. All the sacrifices to his time, diet and lifestyle didn't matter once he stepped onto the ice. But after he'd been injured, he found himself worrying, out of the loop and working hard to stay conditioned for when—and if—he got back in the game. This wasn't the first time he'd been hurt on the ice …but he was afraid it might be his last.

Jenny lifted her steaming cup of hot chocolate, elbows propped on the table, and gently blew on it to cool it, sending the melting whipped cream to the edge of her cup. Dylan could smell the chocolatey sweetness and hint of peppermint. He leaned forward on their tiny square table, trying to think of something to say. It felt as if the awkwardness of last Wednesday's crappy phone call still lingered between them. He wanted to get back to flirting and laughing, but wasn't sure how.

He looked around, noting the tavern was fully decorated for Christmas. Strings of lights lined the long bar, railings, pool tables and trees stood in the corners with wrapped gifts underneath. The waitstaff were also showing their festive enthusiasm with their green-and-red cowboy hats along with Santa Claus print vests.

"It looks like the Ghost of Christmas Future threw up in here."

Jenny, who'd been blowing on her drink, sputtered a laugh, accidentally blowing too hard. The whipped cream splattered across the table, landing on Dylan's suit jacket. He snagged a napkin from the dispenser to surreptitiously wipe at the drops riddling his one sleeve.

"Did I get you? I'm so sorry!" Jenny scrambled for the napkin dispenser, then burst out laughing when she caught the look on his face. Unable to help it, he joined in, letting her unbridled joy for life wash over him.

Jenny came around to his side of the table, fresh napkin in hand. "Let me do it, hon."

"Hon?" He liked the sound of that.

She swiped the napkin down his suit jacket's sleeve, and under her touch, he was tempted to turn his belly toward her like a cat in a sunbeam, craving more.

She enveloped him in a warm hug, quickly slipping away before he had a chance to hold her tight for one brief, wonderful moment. His heart pounded like he'd gone on a rollercoaster ride. 'Hon' and a hug? He was a very lucky man.

"Sorry about your jacket," she said, sitting again.

"You're worse than Rylnn," he joked. He still hadn't gotten all the glitter out of his cast. At least most of the guys on the team had met Ry, so they hadn't ridden him too hard about it or the bits of nail polish he'd failed to properly remove.

"How'd you become a hockey player?" Jenny asked, pushing her hot chocolate aside. "Were you born on skates?"

He chuckled, thinking back to his start. "My parents thought I was getting chunky, so they threw me into hockey."

"No." Her eyes roamed his body. "You lie. I need to see photographic evidence."

"Meet my mom and she'll show you more than you'll ever want to see."

"I like her already. Is she still in Wisconsin where you grew up?" He nodded. "How many teams have you played for?"

Dylan let out a long breath. From pond hockey to the minors to juniors, then on to a farm team and the NHL…it was a lot.

"Okay. How many NHL teams?" she amended.

"Three."

"Favorite team to play for?"

"Don't make me say it."

She leaned across the table, eyes wide as she whispered, "It's not the Dragons? The team that can barely bag a win this year? How can that not be your favorite?"

"Hey! We're a new expansion team still learning how to gel. We're going to rise like the Vegas Knights did."

Her nose crinkled adorably. "Sorry, if it's not football…"

He sighed and shook his head.

"So you've moved a lot for hockey?" she asked.

He nodded. "You? How many places have you lived?"

She held up three fingers. "Lived at home with my parents here in town, then moved into my own place after high school —just above the hardware store in the apartments there. Then recently, Gramps had a fall, so I moved in with him."

He'd changed addresses that many times before he'd even hit puberty.

"Would you ever leave?" he asked.

She shrugged. "I'd like to travel more."

"I travel a lot. It's not all that great."

"Yeah, but it's for work, right?"

He nodded. Depending how the schedule fell during hockey season, he could be in as many as three to four different cities in a week.

"That's not the same. I'd like to go to Spain or on a cruise or…actually, I'm game to go anywhere, really."

"I used to bike everywhere in the Netherlands. I'd love to go back and retrace my old routes."

"I guess on one of our future dates, we'll have to go bike riding in the Netherlands," she said easily, leaning back as the waitress dropped off their plate of wings.

"During tulip season." Which unfortunately was during playoffs, which he always hoped his team would make. If not this year, then next year. Assuming he was still playing.

Still, he could see the two of them riding along the country trails. He'd enjoy showing her his old stomping grounds. It would be relaxing.

An older woman stopped at the table, her feet set wide, as if she was used to stopping animals thrice her size from getting past her. Dylan was pretty sure she was the same woman he'd seen in front of Jenny's earlier, looking at the pink cowboy boots. She slid a folded piece of paper beside Jenny's cup while addressing Dylan. "Sorry to interrupt your meeting."

He nodded politely while shooting Jenny a confused look. She smirked, eyeing his suit jacket. Maybe he did need a wardrobe shift if people thought he was in a meeting and not on a date. Then again, he hadn't planned to wind up in a tavern.

Jenny unfolded the note, calling over her shoulder to the departing woman, "Thank you, Maria."

The woman paused and turned back, saying apologetically, "I don't have her size."

"Santa has helpers," Jenny said, sliding the slip of paper into the front pocket of her jeans.

"Do you ever take time off?" Dylan asked Jenny.

An unfamiliar frown formed. "I told you at Thanksgiving that I'm a small business owner and that I have busy times."

"You need boundaries."

"Excuse me?"

"You let people walk up to you while you're on a date, and put in their Christmas order?" He gestured to Jenny's pocket.

The frown that had been slowly transforming her face into a cloud of displeasure suddenly washed away as though a stiff breeze had whisked in. She burst out laughing. "Just so you know, you're feeling resentful because I'm a secret Santa."

"Oh."

"There's a Christmas hamper program here in town, but there are never enough gifts for teens. So a few people bring me names and I choose something I think will suit them, then get it sent to them through the hampers."

"It's only November. You're starting already?"

"There are only twenty-seven days until Christmas, Dylan!"

He gestured to the pocketed note. "And you know everyone in town?"

"If I don't, I have helpers who track down their size."

"What if they don't like western wear?"

She shrugged. "It's all I carry, really. But jeans are jeans."

He shook his head. They weren't. "I wouldn't be caught dead wearing jeans as tight as a cowboy's."

She laughed.

"What? I have a strong sense of style."

"I admit the fit of your jeans look good on you. Even if they're not tight."

"I'll take that as a compliment."

"It was one."

"So?" he asked. "What else do you do?" He got the feeling there was more than just this clothing hamper thing.

"What do you mean?"

"I know a lot of random things about you, Jenny, who likes tight jeans, trucks, and every animal in the kingdom, including snakes because they make having no legs look cute. She also wants to go to Spain, and as a kid took a free introductory Spanish lesson at the community center in hopes of one day crossing the ocean, preferably as part of a cruise."

"I didn't take Spanish lessons at the community center." A tiny smile quirked her lips. "I learned it from the nurse that helped me with Gramps after his fall. And because you asked, I also cover unpaid bills at the diner. Just the hard luck cases so kids can eat. And then a few other little things." She waved a hand, brushing off her good deeds, unaware she was pulling at his heartstrings.

"How do you afford to do all of that?"

She blushed. "I live with Gramps. My personal expenses are pretty low. And I get clothes at cost."

"Why do you do so much?" He stole the carrot stick from the side of her empty wings plate. "Does everyone around here chip in like that?"

"Well, no." She shrugged, pushing her piece of celery his way. "I just want to help make the town a better place."

Her attention drifted through the tavern as he polished off her vegetables, absorbing what her generosity said about her as a person. She obviously cared a great deal about the people in her life.

"Sweetheart Creek is an incredible community," she said, her voice faraway. "It's home. And it hurts when I see people I think of as family going through a tough time." She folded her arms on the table and leaned forward. "Why wouldn't I help if I could?"

"Community," he echoed. Being on a hockey team was like a smaller version of living in a small town in some ways. That support and feeling of family. If someone needed something, it never was a problem for long because someone would step in, make it right, help out.

If his foot didn't heal and he lost his hockey contract, maybe it wouldn't be the end of the world. Maybe he'd even find what he needed in a place like Sweetheart Creek. Maybe….

* * *

Jenny sucked in a breath and looked away from the couple that had caught her eye.

"What?" Dylan, arms on the small table, pressed against it, leaning closer, making it wobble under his weight.

"Nothing." She blinked and smiled. There was no way she was talking about her ex-boyfriend Ranger Torrington with Dylan. She was still embarrassed whenever she saw Ranger and it had been *years*. He'd seemed like the perfect boyfriend, taking her to football games, out to dinner, saying all the right things and leading her to think they were the real thing. But five months into their relationship, when she'd finally summoned the courage to tell him how she felt, he'd recoiled. It was too soon. They were just having a good time. Didn't she understand that?

No. No, she hadn't.

She also hadn't understood when he'd married someone else less than six months later.

She knew it made her a petty person who was welcoming bad karma, but she'd been deeply satisfied when his marriage hadn't lasted a year.

"You know them?" Dylan asked, looking to the right where Ranger and a woman Jenny didn't recognize were making out like a couple of teenagers.

"Sometimes small towns are a bit too small," she said carefully.

"I sense a story?"

She winced. "Yeah. Let's not go there."

It was probably just a matter of time before someone in the tavern popped by their table to make a remark about how

Ranger was the one who got away, and then she'd have to explain it all to Dylan anyway.

Dylan took a second look and made a face like he'd seen something disturbing.

Unable to resist, Jenny darted a look. The woman had slid into Ranger's lap, his mouth grazing down the side of her neck. The woman tossed her head back in pleasure and Jenny shuddered.

"You aren't into PDA?" Dylan asked.

"That's a bit beyond a public display of affection."

"Obviously he's a good kisser," Dylan said, stealing another look.

"Ha! Hardly." She gulped the last of her cooled hot chocolate. "Ranger went for the neck. Blech."

"What? Is he a vampire?" Dylan joked, clearly not understanding that neck kisses were awkward and weird.

"Getting kissed on the neck isn't sexy."

Dylan angled his head, studying Jenny. "Wait. I know we have our differences…" He splayed his fingers, hand extended, as though he had to calm her down. "But neck kisses are incredibly hot."

"They aren't hot."

"You clearly haven't been kissed right."

Intriguing thought. Could being kissed 'right' make a person weak in the knees like romance novels promised?

Nope. She couldn't see it.

"Neck kisses are for perfume ads, Dylan. Don't get sucked in by the hype."

He choked on a laugh.

"Seriously." She leaned over the table, putting her hand over his and speaking in a hushed whisper. "What are you even supposed to *do* with yourself during a kiss like that?

Stand there like a limp prima donna who's so overcome, she can't stand up any longer?"

Dylan, suddenly serious, was watching her with something burning in his eyes that sent a fleeting image to her mind—of his hands in her hair, taking his time as his lips trailed down her neck.

She shivered. What on earth was *that*?

She pulled back, crossing her arms across her chest. "Not hot."

Okay, so what if she longed to kiss Dylan and maybe let him try a neck kiss? She wasn't going to cause a scene.

"So what do you do other than play hockey?" she asked, desperate to talk about something else so her body would stop its zinging whenever she looked at Dylan's mouth.

He moved toward her. "Where do you like to be kissed?"

"I'm not discussing this with you." Didn't want to imagine it with him, either.

"Why not? You don't want me to kiss you?"

There was a twinkle in his gray eyes, giving them an almost blueish sparkle.

"How is a woman supposed to answer a question like that?"

"With a yes."

She laughed. This man was like nobody she'd ever met. Smooth, but in a way that was completely unintentional.

"Fine," she said with a hint of sassiness. If he did kiss her, she wanted it to be good. The kind of kiss she enjoyed. She tapped the inside of her elbow. "Kiss me here."

"There?" He looked at her as though she'd told him that the callous on her big toe was her most responsive erogenous zone. He tugged her hand across the table and, testing, slid his hand over the fabric of her sleeve, up toward the spot she'd touched. She yanked her hand back, tingles already racing up her arm, the flash of heat in his gaze catching her off guard. "Interesting."

"Yes." She could feel warmth moving into her cheeks as she tugged at her cuff, still feeling the tingles and warmth flowing through her body. She really needed to stop imagining what it would be like to have him prop her up in the privacy of the hallway outside the restrooms and perform a kiss test. Inside the elbow. Side of the neck. Behind the knee, like her friend Cassandra—Rylnn's nanny—swore by... There were so many, many delicious choices.

Lost in her own head, Jenny jumped when she followed Dylan's attention to a man standing beside her.

"Henry!" She placed a hand flat against her chest, addressing the white-haired old man. "You startled me."

Chatting with the town's grumpiest citizen was one way to drop cold water on her libido...

"Your chickens are out," Henry Wylder said gruffly.

"How do you know they're mine?"

"I can go catch 'em for you, but then I'll keep 'em."

"Henry!" Jenny squawked, pulling out her phone to text Gramps. He'd be able to check on her hens. She paused, thumb over her phone's keyboard. It was dark out already. She wasn't sending her eighty-year-old grandfather down the back stairs and into the uneven, poorly lit backyard.

"They're not good for eating, Henry!" Jenny warned. "They're old."

"Good laying hens, I've heard."

She drew in a furious breath, aware he was intentionally riling her up, but was unable to stop her reaction.

Across the table, she realized Dylan was getting just as frustrated. It was as if a storm cloud had rolled in, his mood darkening, his scowl growing. "Don't touch her chickens. We'll go round them up."

Henry drew himself up to his full height with an indignant sniff. "I'm a born and bred rancher who respects the stock of others. I resent the implication that I'd do her livestock any harm."

"Thanks for the heads up, Henry," Jenny said hurriedly as the two men verbally locked horns. She stood, grabbing Dylan's hand and dragged him away.

Around the tavern people were watching, not even pretending that there was something more interesting in the building than what was going on at her table.

Jenny waved to the waitress. "Put it on my tab, please."

Dylan stopped and reached for his wallet, but Jenny tugged his arm with a promise that he could get it next time.

"I told them," Henry called after them, "changing that bylaw to let livestock within the town's limits was a stupid idea!"

"As stupid as his mom skipping her birth control," Dylan muttered, holding the door for Jenny.

A burst of laughter escaped her as she exited the Watering Hole. "Even though you swear neck kisses are sexy, you're not a half-bad date, Dylan O'Neill."

* * *

Dylan followed Jenny onto the street, his eyes drawn to the nip of her blouse high on her waist and then down to the generous flare of her hips in her Western-style jeans. The back pockets had swirls stitched in silver and the threads twinkled in the light above the tavern's door. She slipped into her jacket; the fabric dropping a curtain over his view.

He reached out, helping her with the collar.

"How long were we in there?" he said. Even though sunset was earlier at this time of year, he was still surprised to see how dark it was already.

"It felt like five minutes, didn't it?" Jenny flashed him a smile, and a dog gave a hopeful bark as they passed. "Not now, Rusty."

Dylan paused, petting the dog's short brown fur. "Heya, pal."

He called to Jenny, "Is he lost? Should we bring him home?"

"Nah. He's just doing his thing."

"His thing?" Dylan asked, catching up with Jenny again.

"He loves the stale cheese bread at the Watering Hole. He usually wanders in under the swinging doors to beg for some, but he can't in the winter because they close them up."

Dylan looked back at the tavern. Sure enough, there were two swinging saloon style doors pinned back along the outer wall and an inner wooden slab door closed across the opening.

Jenny did up the buttons of her denim jacket and muttered about a storm as a flicker of lightning lit up the distant sky. The earlier breeze had picked up, bringing the fresh scent of incoming rain.

As they marched up the street, Dylan glanced over his shoulder to ensure the grouchy senior, Henry, hadn't followed them in order to get in a few more licks.

"Do you think he let your chickens out?" Dylan asked.

"Who? Henry?" Jenny frowned at Dylan in the most adorable way. Even frowning, her dimples flashed with cheeriness and a feeling of warmth and safety.

And she gave the best hugs, too. The one he'd received

earlier had been much too quick, but she had generous, rounded curves that had been a heady, addictive mix of acceptance and unconditional belonging. He was definitely smitten. And possibly projecting. Maybe he was lonelier than he'd realized.

If so, he was a prime target for a savvy puck bunny. The smart ones studied the players, then charmed them into believing they were genuine. By the time the guy figured out the woman wasn't really into hockey, or him, she was knocked up and siphoning his paychecks.

All the more reason to fall for a warm and truly genuine woman like Jenny. She reminded him of life before hockey when people treated him normally and not like he was a god on skates.

"Henry's harmless," Jenny stated.

Dylan hopped on his good foot to match shoulders with Jenny again. Not being able to flex his right ankle was slowing him down. Jenny might be short, but she sure could move.

The sky lit up, almost blinding him, and a loud boom of thunder echoed directly above.

"We'd better hurry. It's going to rain," she said.

The streetlights and the glow from storefronts blanked out, plunging them into darkness.

"Seriously? Another outage?" Jenny complained, pulling out her phone. She had it to her ear in seconds, saying, "Is the power out there? I'm heading home right now." A pause. "I know. Just stay put. I don't want you tripping." She sighed, listening to the man on the other end. "Gramps, your new phone has a flashlight. Remember? I showed you. If you have to get up, use it."

She ended the call after a bit more back and forth, then turned on her own phone's flashlight app, her pace brisk.

"Bill keeps chewing through the town's wiring," she said. "I swear, in every storm we lose power these days."

"Who's Bill?" And how was he still alive if he was chomping through live wires?

"A cranky ol' armadillo that the town seems to love." She let out a slightly evil laugh, then leaned her shoulder against his, saying quietly, "He's a four-legged version of Henry, if you ask me."

Dylan shook his head. How many nuances did a town like Sweetheart Creek have? And if he was to move here—hypothetically, of course—how long would it take to feel as though he fit in?

"You okay there?" Jenny slowed her pace.

He straightened his spine. "I'm fine." The word came out gruff, but Jenny simply carried on. "Comes off soon." He gestured in the darkness to his cast.

"It's sounds like a lot of people are waiting to hear how it is."

He swallowed hard, nodding. "It'll be fine."

Although he probably shouldn't still be feeling those twinges where the bones had mended back together along his arch. One tumble at training camp after a hit during floor hockey and he was down for months. So stupid.

"Good. I can tell you love hockey."

"Can you?" he asked, surprised.

She nodded.

"Ever broken a bone?" he asked.

"Nope. Knock on wood." She rapped her knuckles on the top of her head. "When I was a kid, I thought it would be kind of fun. Crutches, a cast, and some extra attention. Now though? Not a chance I'd wish it on myself or anyone else."

As they continued past a storefront that proclaimed it

would soon be a bookstore, he realized it was Athena Gavras's new venture. She and her sister, he'd heard, were opening a shop, even though Athena worked in the city several days a week as the Dragons' dietician. He still couldn't believe that Athena and Jenny used to go to school together. For such a big state, sometimes Texas just felt like one big small town.

"Hey, so you know pretty much everyone in town?" Dylan asked Jenny.

"Not quite. But I know someone everywhere I go and we look out for each other. How about you? Do you have a place like here? Somewhere that feels like home? Or are all the places just hockey pit stops?"

"Yeah, sorta."

"What about your place in San Antonio? Home or pit stop?"

"It's nice." He thought of the two-bedroom townhouse he'd bought when he'd been traded—thanks to Denver's need to keep below their salary cap—and all the landscaping and outdoor living spaces he'd had put into the backyard. He liked it, but it still didn't feel like home. He wasn't sure why. Because he was on the road a lot and never there? Or maybe because he didn't have any pets or a family to come home to?

"It's a pit stop. It's hard to settle in when you know a trade could happen."

"So the talks I read about are pretty serious, then?"

"They are."

"When will it be decided?"

"Once I'm back on the ice." Healed and earning his keep again. And hopefully, still worth every penny the owner, Miranda, had spent to bring him to her team.

"When'll that be?"

"Probably in about two months."

"Cool. So we have some time to play." She flashed him a smile that was picked up by the glow of her phone's flashlight.

"Yeah." He slid his hand into hers, his desire to win her over renewed. She wasn't like most women he met. In fact, he had a feeling she might just be the one he'd been waiting for. But he didn't have the luxury of time on his side. If she was the woman for him, he needed to have her convinced they belonged together before his life got upended.

"So I was reading your bio."

He winced. It was obvious she'd done some checking up on him, but he cringed at the thought of what she might have read. Some bios were an embarrassing string of achievements that made him sound like a superhero. Honestly, he was just an average NHL player who'd worked as hard as he could to get to where he was now.

"It was in a book."

"There's no book."

She giggled, her shoulder bumping against his again. Despite the approaching storm, her pace had become leisurely since he'd taken her hand. "Would you say yes to a book being written about you?"

"There's nothing to tell. I worked hard. Got lucky. Here I am."

"Hm. I bet there's more to it. I read you moved to a California beach town from the Netherlands when you were seven, but you never learned to surf."

"We were only there a few years before settling in Wisconsin."

"Moving to Cali must've been a culture shock. I mean, I understand the Dutch can lean toward being a wait-and-see kind of crowd, but that's a different sort of vibe than you get in a sleepy California coastal town."

Dylan shrugged. It was hard to put his finger on all the reasons he hadn't fit in there. His accent. His rigid decisiveness, his blunt directness, his family's conservative values. He'd been odd in all the wrong ways.

The dairy farm in the Midwest had been a better fit, but by then, he was already who he was. A quiet loner who no longer bothered trying to fit in. Why get his hopes up?

Then he'd started hockey, the sport consuming his life with camps, practices, games and tournaments, then higher-level teams further away until he was in the juniors and trying to make it all work around college classes. Hockey had become his life, the place where he fit.

"I'm at the edge of town," Jenny said, pointing ahead as a drizzle started. "Want to know a secret?"

"Always."

"In my head I call Gramps' place the sugar cookie country house."

"Why?"

"When Gramps and Grams first built it, it was in the country and the town kind of grew around it. Older folks still call it the country house. And since Grams used to bake sugar cookies…" She paused and shrugged.

"Were you two close?"

Jenny nodded. "I used to go over to their place after school when my parents were traveling for their energy consultant business. So basically, all the time. Grams would have sugar cookies ready for me along with a cup of hot cocoa."

"You live with your grandfather, right? Gramps?"

Jenny nodded again, and he had the feeling she was dealing with a pesky lump of emotion caught in her throat. He gave her hand a squeeze, wanting to know more, but not wanting to press.

"Won't be long until the sky opens up," she announced a few moments later. The wind had gotten cold, the drizzle turning into honest rain. And somehow, he didn't care. As long as he was with Jenny, he'd happily stay out here all night.

But he did worry she'd catch a chill once the rain soaked through her jacket. Lightning lit up the sky again, and across the street, he spied his Cadillac, one of the few vehicles along the almost-empty curb.

"Should we drive?"

"Nah, I'm just a couple of blocks over. It'll take the same amount of time." They turned down a residential street, and Jenny stumbled over an uneven bit of sidewalk. Dylan snagged her, pulling her closer to his body than he needed to, inhaling the scent of her shampoo.

She thanked him with a murmur and after another block, Dylan spotted a small moving shape.

"Is that a chicken?" he asked, peering through the rain.

"Might be." Jenny began walking faster.

By the time Dylan caught up with Jenny, she was crawling out from under someone's wet hydrangea with a hen under her arm. She rejoined him on the sidewalk and they crossed the street to a house with a very generous yard, one set further back than the rest of the homes. That was the country house, he'd bet.

Jenny led them up a stone walkway, then skirted the sprawling abode with the big porch, opening a gate at the side of the yellow and white home. A few decorative, solar-powered lights did their best to fight against the consuming darkness brought on by the blackout and rain. But he could tell the backyard was generously-sized. There didn't seem to be any houses behind Jenny's, and possibly no back fence separating her yard from the wilds of Texas Hill Country which sprawled out beyond it. He followed Jenny to a barn-shaped chicken coop with a solar light attached above the door, the scent of rained-upon chicken droppings intensifying as they drew closer.

"Does the power go out much?" he asked.

"Not really."

"Get a deal on solar lights?" They were everywhere.

"It was a joke. Here. Hold her." She thrust the wet and muddy hen into Dylan's arms, then knocked her hip against the wonky wooden coop door, freeing it. She took the chicken back again, setting her inside, then scooped food from a bucket and closed the hutch, jiggling the latch.

"Stupid thing. I need to replace it. My cat keeps busting in to eat their feed, and then the chickens get out." She confirmed the door was secured and all of her hens were in, then gestured to the lights. "For my thirtieth birthday, everyone bought me solar lights. They said my sunny disposition could power them all." She let out an amused huff.

"Sounds like the gifts the guys on the hockey team give."

"Pranksters, huh?"

"You could say that."

"Violet told me Leo got nicknamed Socks? Because of a prank or something?"

Dylan chuckled. "Leo's a rookie."

"Right."

"So, first game of the season he forgot his hockey socks. It was kind of a big deal."

"Couldn't he borrow some?"

"They're part of the uniform. They go over your shin and knee pads."

"I know. Violet explained it to me. But she said he didn't forget them. That someone took them?"

"I wouldn't know anything about that," Dylan said innocently, knowing full well it was one of their forwards, Mullens, who'd hidden the uniform pieces. "Naturally, we covered his locker with baby socks the next day."

"Y'all are awful," Jenny said, giving him a light, playful punch in the arm.

"We are." But he knew Leo had taken the ribbing in stride, understanding it meant he was accepted as one of the team.

Dylan was really going to miss those guys when he finally had to hang up his skates. He couldn't quite visualize what it would be like to no longer be one of the guys. Would he spend his days fretting over his investment properties and growing fat? He shook his head. There was time enough to think about that later.

He slipped his hand in Jenny's again, wishing tonight could last forever.

* * *

Jenny, feeling slightly giddy from her date, huddled on the country house's porch with Dylan, wondering if her grandfather would come out and chase him off before he could kiss her. She hoped not, but she also wasn't sure how much longer she could handle the chill that was working through her wet clothing and into her bones.

She could invite Dylan in, out of the drumming rain, but she wasn't ready to introduce him to Gramps. Not yet. Plus, because of the blackout, they'd be hanging out by candlelight, needlessly chaperoned by a snoopy, opinionated eighty-year-old. That would be a sure way to chase Dylan away.

Still, she needed to go in and check on Gramps.

But she wanted a kiss.

Desperately.

She opened the door, hollering inside, "Gramps, I'm home, but I'm going to be a minute. You okay?"

"I haven't fallen!" His tone was sharp, frustrated by either the darkness or her fussing. It could be either one, but it was probably the latter.

She closed the door again with an apologetic smile to Dylan, who had propped one hand against the doorjamb when she'd leaned inside. He didn't move, creating a cave for her between his body and the door. He smelled like the night air, and he enveloped her in some very welcoming heat.

"Hey," he said, his voice low, rough like gravel. She shivered, partly from anticipation and partly from the chill.

"You cold?" He was eyeing her outfit, his gaze tracing lines across her hips and chest.

"Yes."

He rubbed his free hand down her arm, the faint light from his phone's flashlight highlighting what looked like a zip of heat in his blue-gray eyes. He blinked it away so quickly, she could brush it off as imagined.

She'd never thought of herself as the type of woman a man like him might go for. She'd always felt as though her curviness was something a man would decide to settle for, because the rest of her was more than enough. But with Dylan and the way he looked at her, her curves felt like one of the many things he was happily checking off his preferences checklist.

Dylan was still close, and a drop of rain fell from his hair, landing on her cheek. He brushed the water away and she shivered, uncertain of what to make of his tenderness.

She held her breath, her chest tight, caught on the threshold, not quite ready to let go and pull him against her like she wanted to, but not quite ready to let the opportunity slip past her, either. They were opposites, their worlds never destined to collide in the way she wanted them to.

"We're so incompatible," she whispered, immediately cursing herself for the mood-breaking comment.

"We are?"

"We're opposites. You like neck kisses. Any ravaging would surely be a one-sided disappointment."

"Disappointment? Really?"

Hesitantly, she lifted a hand, resting it against his wide, damp chest. He tilted his head at just the right angle for a kiss.

She took a step back as a sudden bout of nerves hit her, bumping her head on the doorjamb just below Dylan's hand.

"Do I make you nervous?" There was a hint of amusement in his voice, as if he was aware he was unsettling her...and he liked it.

"Most men would have kissed me or left by now."

He chuckled. "And you like most men?"

"I like inside elbow kisses, country music and smiling."

"I smile."

"Barely."

"I think we have more in common than you think. And I'm positive that you could come to like neck kisses."

"You're delusional." The doorjamb was pressing into her spine.

"I thought you were more open-minded. More adventurous."

"I am," she said. She was also very impatient to be kissed, but there was no way she was going first. Not with him.

She was ready for adventure, eager for something scrapbook-worthy to happen in her life. Something she could tuck away forever, like a kiss from an NHLer who made her feel alive. When she was Gramp's age, married to some rancher she'd eventually meet, she'd pull out this kiss and replay it with a smile, knowing she'd experienced some adventures.

The rain suddenly quieted on the porch roof and Jenny shivered again.

She tipped her head to the left, exposing her neck. "Fine. Give it a shot. But neck kisses?" She scoffed. "You're *never* going to change my mind."

"We'll see." He pocketed his phone, the flashlight creating a bright spot of blue in the front of his jeans.

"You forgot to turn off your light."

His focus was strictly on her, uninterested in anything but moving closer. She was gently pinned between the doorjamb and his body, but he wasn't touching her yet. She could move away. Escape. Laugh it all off.

But there was no way she ever would.

She placed both palms against his chest, her chilled fingers welcoming the heat pouring through his shirt.

She was starting to think he was messing with her, and a memory from a junior high dance flashed through her brain. At the end of a slow song with Ryan Wylder, she'd tipped up on her toes to kiss him, but he'd quickly stepped away, looking relieved to be escaping.

She shook off the memory. This wasn't junior high. Dylan was interested. He was going to kiss her.

Eventually.

"Well?" she asked, her breathiness betraying her.

"Be patient," he mumbled, his tone grumpy. His hands rested lightly on her shoulders, then moved to trace a gentle trail up her neck. His fingers glided into her hair, loosening her already disheveled ponytail. She felt it fall from its elastic, tumbling in wet strands around her face.

She probably looked a mess, but she felt sexy. *Wanted.*

She swallowed hard, aware that she already felt as though she'd been thoroughly kissed.

His head lowered, as if he was going to whisper in her ear, and she automatically lifted her cheek, giving him access. His fingers brushed the hair away from her neck, then stole a spot at her waist. He brought their bodies close, his breath warm on her exposed skin.

She swallowed, waiting for his lips to connect, the anticipation feeling like the most erotic thing she'd ever experienced. Instead, his mouth gently grazed a trail down the cords of her neck to the spot where they met her collarbone. His breath was hot, shiver-inducing. A shower of goosebumps danced across her skin. Her body arched toward him, her chest pressing into his.

Want. Need.

What was this man doing to her?

Her hands gripped Dylan's dress shirt as his mouth trailed lazily, torturously, back up her neck to the spot under her jawbone where her pulse quickened. His lips landed and he finally kissed her, gently sucking the skin as though he had all the time in the world. Her eyes closed, her eyelids felt drawn together as though by magnets. Shivers chased each other through her nervous system and her body awakened after a slumber so long, she wondered if she'd ever truly been awake.

He broke the kiss, his body's warmth retracting as he stepped away.

"Good night, Jenny."

She nodded mutely and fell into the dark house on weak legs.

He was right.

Neck kisses were the sexiest thing she'd ever experienced. And maybe so, too, was Dylan O'Neill.

CHAPTER 5

"These are for the hampers." Dylan set a stack of gift cards on Blue Tumbleweed's counter beside Jenny's tablet which served as a cash register. He set down another pile, then another, sending the tinsel taped to the counter fluttering. There were cards for grocery stores, gas stations, and cool stores in San Antonio that he'd heard teenagers liked.

He hoisted one of the shopping bags he'd carried in. "Toys. I've got more in the car."

Jenny was blinking, speechless. He'd broken her, apparently.

"Am I too late for Secret Santa or whatever it's called?" he asked. It was only December 1. He couldn't possibly have missed it.

Jenny seemed to come to life, shaking her head, her bangs brushing her brows.

"When did you get bangs?"

"I was bored yesterday." She pulled at the strands covering her forehead.

"Power was still out?"

"Let's not talk about it."

He bit back a smile. "Well, for the record, I think they're cute." She was wearing a green elf-print headband and looked entirely kissable.

Her cheeks turned pink and she frowned as though concentrating. "This is all for the Secret Santa hampers?"

"Yes."

She sorted through the piles as he reached into his Dragon jacket's inside pocket. On Saturday, he'd learned a twelve-hundred-dollar lesson on not wearing a suit jacket when coming to see Jenny on her own turf. Although, truthfully, the jacket wasn't destroyed. It just needed a cleaning. This time.

He pulled out a stack of narrow Dragons branded folders containing tickets to future home games along with concession vouchers. He laid them in front of Jenny.

"I can't believe you did all of this." She picked up a folder, opening it and studying the contents.

"I didn't." He tapped the tickets. "Daisy-Mae got these."

"But you asked her for them? Made a pitch and all of that?"

"I did."

Jenny exhaled in what seemed to be relief. "Good."

"Why?"

"Well, it might look like nepotism otherwise. You know, using the team to help out people in her hometown."

"I didn't think of that." Daisy-Mae, Maverick's girlfriend, was a local who'd started with the Dragons at the end of September as the mascot handler, helping Violet—dressed in the Dezzie the Dragon costume—around the arena. She was now also a manager for ticket holder experiences, so it had been a no-brainer to ask her to get involved in donating items for the hampers. It was a win-win. They could help people in town while drumming up interest and support for their hockey team. But he hadn't even considered a possible nepotism angle.

"And the rest was you?" Jenny confirmed.

He nodded.

She was staring at him like she wasn't quite sure what to make of it all.

He was now realizing, seeing it all in one pile, that maybe he'd gone a bit overboard in his attempt to show her that they had similar values. And that he understood about being part of a community and helping out when possible.

"Is this okay?" he asked.

Her eyes turned a lighter color and her grin lit up the entire room, hitting him in the solar plexus with the severity of its powerful force. She was around the counter in a flash, enveloping him in a hug that was somehow even better than the moment he'd given her that wonderful neck kiss that had made her shiver and melt.

"It's more than okay!" She squeezed him tight and he inhaled her hair, locking in the memory so he could bring it up later, to enjoy at his leisure. "This is amazing!"

She stepped back, still beaming. "I'll make sure you're mentioned as a donor. I think they do up a poster or something."

"Don't you dare."

She raised her eyebrows.

"I'm an elf. Nobody acknowledges elves."

"You sure?"

"Please."

"Okay." She stuck out her hand, as if wanting to shake his. He slowly put out his right hand and she enveloped it, giving it a quick pump. "You're a very welcomed addition to the secret elf collective, Mr. Grumps—"

"Mr. Grumps?"

"But be warned that you are definitely in dangerous territory. You could soften this old cowgirl's heart, and I'm more woman than most men can handle."

"I'll have to try harder then."

She laughed as she made her way back to her station behind the counter. "I look forward to that."

So did he.

"How many of us are there?"

"How many what?" she asked, sorting through the gift cards.

"Elves."

She paused a beat. "Two."

He crossed his arms to hide his secret delight that he was in cahoots with her and nobody else. "Are there meetings?"

"Weekly. Actually, twice a week."

He grunted. "I have a work schedule, too, you know. That's a lot."

"But with Christmas coming up so soon… I can't tell you *how* many last-minute meetings there might be for the collective." She dragged out her words as though they were very weighty.

"I hate meetings."

Her grin was wicked, eyes sparkling. "I promise these ones will be fun."

* * *

"Jenny! Will you sponsor us?" At noon, on Monday, four

adorable eleven-year-olds with front teeth too big for their faces blocked the door to Gramps' house.

She shifted her takeout bags holding lunch and looked at their pledge sheet, still buoyed from Dylan's impromptu visit and incredible generosity.

"What have we got here?" Water wells in the Sudan. "Wait. Aren't y'all supposed to be at school right now?"

"It's lunch break," one explained enthusiastically. "Mrs. Elm said whoever raises the most money gets to sit out of one class from now until Christmas break!"

"And we can win candy!" added another.

"Wow. I'd better sponsor y'all then." She filled out their sheets, sponsoring all four. "Do you get to go to Africa and build the wells? That would be kind of cool, don't you think?"

The kids laughed, not realizing she was serious. Sure, it would be hard work, but it would be more than gratifying to help improve the lives of others. Maybe she should go do it one day. Once April had her baby and had returned to Blue Tumbleweed, possibly Jenny could slip away for a few weeks. She could even have someone like Athena check in on Gramps for her.

By then Dylan would probably be traded away—possibly back to his former team in Denver. Meanwhile, Jenny would be bored in Sweetheart Creek again, sad and no doubt missing him and in need of a massive distraction.

Earlier that morning, relationship-wise, Dylan had been firmly in a wait-and-see category. Jenny had been unsure if Saturday night's sneak peek into her real life had scared him off—taverns, country music, the fact that she cared for and lived with her grandfather, blackouts caused by armadillos and then chasing escapee chickens in the rain. Never mind the fact that she'd no doubt cost him some dry-cleaning for his possibly ruined suit jacket, first with the whipped cream splatters, then the mud when she'd thrust Saratoga at him while she'd fixed the coop's door. She hadn't been thinking, but she'd been herself, and if he didn't like that, then, well… So be it.

But then he'd walked into her store two hours ago, blowing her mind with his incredible support for her community.

The kids, still giggling, trundled down the front steps, cutting across the lawn to go hit up Gramps' neighbor, Ryan Wylder, who was likely out at his family's ranch or with his girlfriend Carly.

Jenny let herself into her grandfather's house, calling out, "I've got lunch!"

"In here."

She followed his voice through the main floor to the kitchen overlooking the backyard and Texas hills that stretched beyond as far as she could see. Gramps, tall, his back bent by age, turned from the sink where he'd been washing the breakfast dishes. He hoisted his jeans, which were held up by suspenders.

"Look at you," he said, his bushy white eyebrows dancing.

"What about me?" Jenny glanced down at her aquamarine shirt with the beaded rose, matching Kickapoo necklace, worn Wranglers and pink boots. She loved this outfit. It made her feel good. Hopeful. And today she'd been hoping to see Dylan again.

And he'd appeared.

This outfit was magic.

"You really like him," her grandfather said.

Jenny felt her face flush. "Who?"

"Still smiling two days after your date." He pulled out a kitchen chair and sat. "How does he vote? Is he a keeper?"

Jenny laughed, setting down the bag of food from the Longhorn Diner. Her neck still burned thinking about how hot Dylan's Saturday night kiss had been and wishing she'd been able to angle another one out of him before he'd had to slip back to the city for work this morning.

"Hold your horses, Gramps. It was one date."

"NHLers have to fall in love with someone, you know. Don't cross him off your list just yet."

She sighed, passing him a burger from the bag. "Apparently, he's kind of a big deal in hockey and there are trade talks. So even if something were to happen between us..." She sighed again, shoving her burger in her mouth and wishing the food could bury her conflicted feelings about Dylan.

"What? You're stuck here? You can't chase him across the country if he moves?"

"He could be traded to *Canada*, Gramps. They have winter there! Like, real winter. And it goes on for months and months."

"So buy a coat."

She mumbled into her burger, "I can't leave Sweetheart Creek."

"Why? Did you have a run-in with Sheriff Johnson you're not telling me about?"

"What?"

"All this can't-leave-town business. What's up with that?"

Jenny laughed. "Gramps! I meant because of my responsibilities and stuff. This is home. You don't just up and leave it all for some guy because he makes you feel special."

Gramps stared at her for a long moment, then shoved a bunch of fries, slathered in ketchup, into his mouth.

"Better to play it safe and break it off now, then?" he mumbled.

"You don't think I deserve some fun? Not everything has to lead down the aisle, you know," she retorted, giving him a pointed look while throwing April's argument at him.

She was a good granddaughter, and a good daughter, too. Her parents were still traveling the world with their alternative power consulting work instead of being here, taking care of Gramps. And her brothers were busy off having their own families. Just because she took care of people, that didn't mean she didn't want a life of her own.

"Thatta girl!" Gramps crowed, and she realized his question had been meant to rile her up.

"He's got to be deranged, though. To think the way I talked back to him at Thanksgiving was an invitation to come back for more?" It still surprised her that he had come back. It tickled her in a way that made her want to smile twenty-four-seven.

Her grandad chuckled. "I like him already."

She leaned forward, elbow on the table. "And there's more to like. Did you know he showed up this morning with gift cards for the Christmas hampers that are worth a couple grand?"

"How would I have heard about that? I thought you were doing it all in secret?"

"I am. But anyway, he did." He was love bombing her, lavishing generosity to encourage positive thoughts and feelings about him.

But she didn't care. She knew what she was getting into this time. Nothing serious. Just two adults looking to have some fun together.

"So I made him a member of the secret elf collective."

"What on God's green earth is that?"

"A name for the stuff I do with the hampers."

Her grandfather harrumphed. "Missed opportunity, if you ask me."

"What do you mean?"

"Could've called it the Secret Elves of Xmas."

"That's cute."

"And it makes for a better acronym."

Jenny spelled it out in her mind and, as it clicked, her grandpa waggled his eyebrows.

"Gramps!"

"Correct me if I'm wrong, but isn't that what you're looking for?"

"We need to find you a girlfriend," she muttered.

Her grandfather had been alone for almost fifteen years since Grams' passing. Recently, for some reason Jenny couldn't understand, he'd focused his charms on Fiona Fisher, the Longhorn's main server, who was a married woman. Fiona had then introduced Gramps to her twin sister, and the two had dated passionately—Jenny had been spared no details —but they'd recently broken up.

When Gramps had been in a relationship, Jenny had been able to relax a bit, not having to worry about him all the time. It had given her time to explore her own interests, and to wonder where her life was heading. But now she was back to being his number one contact when he had a problem. She didn't mind, but it hadn't been the way she'd expected these last few months to pan out.

"Lots of fish in the sea," Gramps said, finishing his fries with a self-satisfied smile.

"Oh, hey. Did you take our new neighbor that batch of

sugar cookies I baked? I meant to do it this morning before work."

Gramps shook his head.

"Be neighborly for me? Welcome her. Cookies are on the counter."

"Is this because she looks about my age?" he asked, bushy eyebrows raised.

"Nope," she lied. "But if something happens, it happens." She winked and finished her burger, trying to imagine what it might be like if she and Dylan became a thing. What would it be like dating a pro athlete? From where she stood, it seemed as though her friend Daisy-Mae Ray was insanely busy keeping up with team captain Maverick. But she was also working two new jobs in San Antonio and commuting every day. Plus, she was also helping Maverick with publicity stuff that Jenny figured his agent or someone else should have been doing for him.

Honestly, it didn't look at all how she imagined the way things would go for her and Dylan. He'd be on the road a lot, for sure. The press might hound them here and there, but probably not if she and Dylan hung out in Sweetheart Creek. They might also do things like take trips together and dine in fancy restaurants like McKenzie's, where she'd get to dress up.

For Dylan, she'd go find the perfect outfit if it killed her. And it might. She cringed, just thinking of going into someone else's store and trying on everything on the rack. Even when dress after dress made her look as if she was the wrong shape, and she received knowing looks from skinny sales staff as she rejected garment after garment.

Everyone believed she'd started Blue Tumbleweed because she was into clothes. In reality, she'd just been so fed up with trying to find something that fit her right that she'd decided having her own shop was the ticket.

Either way, she wasn't looking a gift horse in the mouth when it came to Dylan. The man made her feel beautiful. Plus, he gave very good neck kisses and she was eager to see what one on the lips would feel like.

She was going to take everyone's advice—to enjoy the here and now and stop worrying about the future. If things got serious and lasted between them, they'd figure it out then. Right now, they both just needed an adventure. And she definitely needed one.

CHAPTER 6

*D*ylan had shown up for the first meeting of Jenny's secret elf service, or whatever she'd called it, only to find her dressed all in black and bouncing on her toes in anticipation.

"Perfect timing," she said, pushing a box into his arms.

"I have an away game tomorrow," he warned. It was nearly ten-thirty on a Sunday night which meant he wouldn't get home until well after midnight. Honestly, he probably shouldn't have driven all the way out to Sweetheart Creek at this hour when he had to be at a game the next day. But what man wouldn't make an hour-plus drive when the woman he wanted invited him over?

"You don't actually have to play, so stop complaining. I mean, are you an elf or not?"

He gave her his best scowl. "We really have to do it this late at night?"

"We're putting the secret into secret elf. Everyone will see us if we deliver the hampers in the daylight, silly."

She made a good point, he supposed. And if he was going

to convince Jenny they were more alike than different, spending time with her would surely help.

She shot him a sunny smile. "Chop, chop. Let's go. Besides, you've already driven all this way," she said quietly, stepping past him with a sealed box of her own. He glanced inside the entry to the country house and spied a stack of at least a dozen boxes.

The rest of the house appeared to be in darkness, and based on the way Jenny was moving and speaking, Dylan figured her grandfather had already called it a night.

When they'd transferred all the boxes to her truck, he awkwardly climbed into the passenger seat. His cast was a pain in the butt. It was due to come off in two days—maybe he could remove it tonight and see how it felt?

Yeah, he'd never have the guts to risk it. Not with hockey on the line.

Jenny hopped up into the driver's seat, her black long-sleeve shirt and thin vest hugging her curves. She flashed him a sunny smile as she cranked the engine, then the cab plunged into darkness.

They drove a few blocks before she pulled to a stop. She pointed to a house across the street. "That one." Its shingles were peeling up, ready to be retired from their job of protecting the home from unrelenting weather. She gestured to the backseat. "It doesn't matter which box. Just be quiet and don't wake anyone up."

"Got it. Putting the 'secret' in secret elf." He shed his Dragons jacket, knowing he'd be easy to identify if someone saw him or had a doorbell camera that recorded motion.

He grabbed a box from the back.

"Whatever you do, don't get noticed," Jenny warned.

Dylan walked to the front door, the box in his arms. He set

the package against the door, then carefully made his way back down the creaking wooden steps. From inside he could hear a dog growl, then bark. He increased his pace, his heart hammering harder than it ever did in training. Coach could send him around the rink in sprints for hours and his heartrate would never reach this number of beats per minute. He glanced over his shoulder, checking for moving curtains or other signs that the owner had awakened and decided to look outside.

The next house was in a similar state of disrepair and with each new delivery, his ability to avoid potential creaky steps increased.

"I feel like a teenager pulling pranks," he admitted after the eighth stop. "You've got me afraid we'll get caught."

Jenny said offhand, "Don't worry so much. Everyone knows I deliver the hampers."

He turned to her. "So why don't you drop them off in the daylight?"

She shrugged, then grinned. "This is more fun."

By the time they reached the last drop-off, a house with a Christmas tree lit up in the front window, they had a rhythm going. Jenny would pull up as close as possible, idling the truck while he jumped out to make the delivery.

It was close to midnight as they headed back to Jenny's, Dylan feeling energized despite the late hour. The town was asleep, with very few lights still on, but a motion light high-lighted the front step of one of the first houses they'd visited. Dylan slowed. He pointed and Jenny's gaze followed his finger.

Something waddled away from the hamper they'd left, dragging what looked like a box of noodles.

"No," Jenny said, stopping the truck. "No way."

She hopped out and marched down the sidewalk, hissing and waving her arms. Dylan followed, wondering if the noodles were worth a wildlife run-in.

The animal scurried faster, its body waddling, the dry noodles rattling in their box. Dylan caught up with Jenny as she came around the side of the house where a beautiful rose garden sat like a sentinel, blocking them from following the armadillo who slipped behind a small playhouse.

The front door opened, and the metallic click of a shotgun loading echoed through the silent night.

Dylan reacted, pulling Jenny into the playhouse. They sent two small chairs and its table clattering and banging as they went.

"Shh!" Dylan hissed.

Jenny snorted. "So busted!"

"Shh!"

Jenny curled into a seated ball against his hip and they faced each other, crammed in, safe. For now.

Whoever said small town life was boring was dead wrong.

"That was Bill," Jenny whispered.

"With the shotgun?"

"No, the armadillo. He's the one who chews the town's power lines."

"Shh!"

In the darkness of the playhouse, she found his hand, linking their fingers and giving his a squeeze. She seemed to be shaking, but not from fear. He had a feeling she was holding back laughter.

There was a knock against the side of the playhouse and he jumped involuntarily. "Jenny? That you?"

"Yes, Mrs. Filmore."

"Well then. When you two are done making out in there, come in for a cup of tea and a cookie."

* * *

Jenny waited on the front walk for Dylan after their tea and cookies with Mrs. Filmore. She'd brought out the sugar cookies Jenny had left with her that morning, and between the three of them, they'd made a sizeable dent in the Christmas baking.

It had been amazing to see how Dylan's slightly gruff exterior had softened during the visit—especially after Mrs. Filmore revealed she only had a shotgun recording and not an actual weapon. She claimed she wasn't spry enough to handle something with that much kick any longer, then laughed long and hard about it. He'd visibly relaxed, even under the barrage of Mrs. Filmore's rapid-fire questions about him, his life, his upbringing and all the rest of it. He'd answered quickly and succinctly. Finally, she'd leaned back and declared him a good man.

Now Dylan was standing on the step, waiting to hear the deadbolt slide across on Mrs. Filmore's door, securing her inside.

"Good night, Mrs. Filmore!" he called loudly so she could hear him through the thick slab of wood.

"Don't be a stranger, honey!" her voice hollered back.

Seemingly satisfied, he joined Jenny on the walk and pointed to her truck. "We left the doors open."

It was true. Her vehicle was sitting open with the key inside. "Oops."

He shook his head once, a soft smile toying at his mouth. "Gotta love small towns."

There was a warmth to his statement and Jenny hugged herself, feeling the blessing of her little community. If she left here, she would miss this. And she would miss Dylan, too, when his career took him elsewhere, as it was destined to do. He fit himself into her slice of life moments and it made her want to freeze time, wrap her arms around him and never let him go.

Jenny jumped up into the driver's seat and turned to Dylan who was stifling a yawn. "Hey, do I need to be worried?"

"About what?"

"About Mrs. Filmore. I saw you flirting."

He let out a grunt that sounded pleased and she noted how the visit had relaxed the usual tension that rested in his jaw and shoulders. "She reminds me of my grandma."

"Is that why you ate almost *all* of her cookies?"

"She doesn't take no for an answer."

"Wait until I tell Athena what you did!" she crowed.

"You wouldn't!" Dylan came alive, his eyes wide.

"That was a lot of cookies for someone who's in training. Although, my sugar cookies *are* fantastic. So really, you can't be blamed."

"Too many sprinkles, not enough butter."

Jenny steered the truck toward her house, eyebrows lifted. "Think you can do better?"

"As it happens, yes."

She shook her head as she parked in the driveway.

"Is Christmas baking part of your secret elf missions?"

"Nah. I just like to bake." Jenny patted her hips. "Gramps and I can't afford to eat everything I make."

"I think you can." In the soft light from the streetlight at the curb, she saw heat in his eyes as he studied her curves, drinking her in. Ooh, that was a heady feeling. She gripped the steering wheel, trying to recall if she'd ever been looked at like that before. As if she was a sugar cookie, ready to be devoured.

"Don't carve away what makes you womanly," he said, opening his door, his voice gruff.

Jenny's breathing staggered slightly, and she blinked a few times. "There you go, making me want to fall for you when this is simply a fun adventure," she whispered to herself before he opened the door for her. She shot him a big smile and jumped from the truck. She patted his chest and headed to the house, assuming he'd follow. "If you want my recipe, just ask."

"You won't be saying that once you've tried *my* sugar cookies," he said, walking beside her.

She snorted, unlocking the front door to Gramps' house. "You're going to have to put your money where your mouth is, Buster." She shouldered the door, cracking it ajar, listening for a moment.

Gramps was still asleep. She closed the door before hearing a soft meow, then a light pawing sound. She opened the door a crack, letting her gray cat, Fifty—found by April's husband Brant Wylder in a box of romance novels—to slip out before closing it again.

Dylan announced, "Bake-off."

"Yeah?" She leaned into him, hands on his chest, head tipped back. She was heady with the scent of him, the sugar, the late night, and wondering what he might do with those lips of his. "When?"

"Next date. You'll see how superior my recipe is and you'll never go back to too many sprinkles."

"You're mighty cocky." She pushed away, but he caught her hands, keeping her in place.

"Afraid you'll lose?"

She laughed. "Not at all. I *like* sprinkles."

"They hide the flavor."

"My, you're particular."

"I am."

"We're keeping our dates rather untraditional, aren't we? No wining and dining."

"Is that what you want?" He held her close, his voice low. "Wining and dining?"

She bet he'd pull out all the stops if she nodded. And yet, that wasn't what she wanted at all. Travel, yes. Adventures and fun, also yes. But mostly, she wanted someone to share those adventures, doing things together, helping others... And hopefully kissing. Lots and lots of kissing.

"Actually...I kind of like this," Jenny said, toying with the zipper on Dylan's Dragon jacket. He'd slipped it on as they came up the walk and it looked good on him, emphasizing his broad shoulders and narrow waist, reminding her he was an athlete in his prime. "It's been a lot of fun."

"That's my personal motto."

"Yeah?"

"I have it on a crest above my fireplace."

She stared at him. "Are you joking around Dylan O'Neill? Why, I never knew you had it in you!"

The corners of her lips were twitching, ready to burst out a laugh, but she held back, not wanting to break this spell they were under.

His hands settled on her hips, and she noted how comfortable she was with him. It felt natural and easy. Around them, the night was quiet, with nothing but the faint sound of her cat, Fifty, purring as he rubbed against their legs. Christmas lights danced on houses up and down the street, twinkling merrily in multiple colors.

This was bliss. And having Dylan all to herself meant that any potential distractions had long ago called it a night. They were alone. Figuring out whether they belonged together.

"When does our bake-off date start?" Dylan asked.

"When are you available?"

"Now."

She swore the corner of his mouth lifted into an almost-smile as she replied by opening the front door and inviting him inside.

* * *

It was the middle of the night and Jenny was baking with a professional athlete in her grandfather's kitchen as if it was a totally normal thing to do. They were trying to be quiet so as not to wake up Gramps, but every once in a while, Dylan made her laugh. Trying to hush herself only added to the fun.

There was only one dark spot—Dylan hadn't kissed her tonight. Not once. Not in the playhouse when she'd cozied up to him, and not at the door when they'd been saying good night.

The only kiss they'd shared was that hot neck kiss eight days ago. This was technically another date. Their third. And yet, no kiss. Were they settling into the friend zone?

She didn't want another friend. She had plenty.

"Hey," she said, interrupting Dylan as he used a metal spoon to cream the butter and sugar for his cookie recipe. It was an official sugar cookie bake-off with two very biased judges. She was making her recipe, and he was making his.

Dylan looked up, his serious expression softening as he met her gaze.

"I never got a kiss at the end of our date tonight."

His body language quieted as he leaned against the counter, his eyes looking extra gray thanks in part to the color-matching tee hugging his chest and biceps. She held her breath, waiting for the moment of truth as his gaze locked on hers.

Without seeming to move, he closed the distance, his hands gently framing her face as he lined up their lips. His mouth landed softly, partially open. He took his time, nothing hurried. Then his lips pulled at hers and his tongue darted out, sweeping gently over her lower lip before connecting with hers.

Damp lips. Sugar and butter filling the air. A warm body pressed to hers.

He broke the kiss, his fingers splayed in her hair, his gaze quietly set upon her.

"More?" he whispered.

She nodded silently, her words gone.

He kissed her again, his hands shifting. One slid off the elastic that held her ponytail. He loosened her locks with a gentle tug, sending shivers down her spine. He was tender, but in control. Dominant and yet giving. She didn't feel like she was losing anything; she had just as much power as he did and she deepened the kiss, their bodies using each other for support.

He broke the kiss and she gasped for breath.

He lowered his forehead to hers while their breathing regulated. She whispered, "I'm so glad I asked."

He angled his head, giving her another soft kiss.

She smiled, allowing him to see the impact he had on her.

She'd played it small in relationships so many times, worried that she was going to frighten away her boyfriend with the power of her emotions. But she'd decided, after the fiasco with Ranger, that life was too short to live small. Too short to hold back, to live at half power for someone else's sake. If Dylan couldn't handle her, it was better to know now, not after she developed feelings for him.

She watched Dylan's expression, keeping her arms around his trim, tight waist. His lips softened into a smile of his own, a tiny upturn that caused creases at the corners of his eyes. She'd never seen anything as handsome as those fine lines of contented happiness.

* * *

This woman was breaking his heart. Dylan snatched Jenny's wrist, holding her still.

"What?" Her eyes, green with happiness, looked up at him.

He sighed. "Way too many sprinkles."

"But they're pretty." She pouted, looking down at her row of sprinkle-laden creations. The counter was filling up with cookies, colored sprinkles crunching underfoot whenever he edged closer to Jenny so their elbows or shoulders rubbed while they baked.

"You won't be able to taste the cookie." He let go of Jenny's wrist and freed the jar of tiny, pink star decorations from her grip. Then he set it down with a thunk and abruptly brushed the excess sprinkles from a row of her cookies, smearing icing and coating his hand.

Her jaw dropped in shock. Then she bent her knees and hip-checked him like a seasoned NHLer, sending him to the left as he stumbled to regain his balance. She planted her feet in front of her cookies and narrowed her eyes at him. "My cookies, my sprinkles, my choice. Back off."

He regained his balance and composure, fighting a smile of surprised pleasure.

"Jenny Oliver," he asked, voice dangerously low, "did you just get physical with me?"

"You crossed a line, O'Neill." She let out an indignant huff, her spine straightening.

He wanted to pin her against the counter, untie that stupid chicken-print apron and kiss her until her knees gave out.

She grabbed a jar of red and green sprinkles, a defiant look in her eyes, and he held his breath. She swung her arm over her row of cookies, watching him as her hand slowly tilted the sprinkle jar.

He sighed as the first sprinkle hit the wet icing, sticking to the cookie.

"I like pretty things," she said matter-of-factly. "And I think as punishment, you should have to eat all the cookies you just ruined."

He shook his head. She was going to break him as well as his diet. And strangely enough, he didn't care nearly as much as a man in his position probably should.

Jenny had set down the sprinkles and grabbed one of the icing bags. She'd painstakingly made two types of icing. A thicker version she squeezed in a thin line around the perimeter of her cookie. Then a runnier version, which she then used to "flood" the inside surface, as if the cookie was an ice rink, creating a perfect, smooth layer that quickly hardened. But not before she blasted it with so many sprinkles his head echoed with the crunching sound at the thought of taking a bite.

"You're ruining the cookies," he warned.

"No," she said with practiced patience, "I am bringing the cookie to an all-new culinary level." She glanced at his stack of undecorated, freshly baked cookies. "You going to decorate those? Or are you a cookie nudist?"

"Nudist." He crossed his arms and swallowed. "All the way."

"There is something seriously wrong with you," she muttered.

He had to admit her flooding thing did look fun. Especially when she swirled a bit of food coloring through white icing, creating a professional-looking end product.

She drew a green circle of thinner icing over a flooded cookie. Then flicked a toothpick through the circle, bending and bleeding the color and forming a design.

She held it up for him to see. "Look. An elf."

"Cool." He grabbed the cookie, popping it in his mouth.

"Hey!"

"Shh! You'll wake up your grandpa," he said in a stage whisper.

It was approaching 3 AM and he should have headed home a long time ago. But whenever he considered leaving, they took another kissing break. They'd burned two batches of cookies, thanks to the distraction, and the kitchen now had a faint scorched sugar smell.

At one point Jenny had made coffee, which meant he was fully caffeinated. Still, tomorrow was going to be a train wreck. But oddly enough, he realized he didn't care. Not even when he thought about the lectures he'd get from Coach Louis, and the team's physical therapist, Karlene.

Jenny handed him a piping bag, half-filled with icing, and shot him a smile so bright he forgot about everything but her. "Let's decorate, babe."

He set the bag down. "Nope."

She pressed it back into his hand, guiding him toward his stack of pristine, undecorated treats. "Think of how happy it's going to make some kids when they see these colorful, pretty cookies."

"Think of the sugar rush, Jenny. It's irresponsible."

Her lips curved upward as she shook her head with a humored snort. She set a row of blank cookies in front of him, sensing he'd already caved despite his protests.

Obediently, he squeezed the icing onto the surface of the first cookie, his handiwork wiggly and uncertain. At this point, Jenny could probably ask him to go purse shopping with her and he'd happily comply.

Some men were happy to follow their woman anywhere, and apparently, he was one of them.

He shook his head. He was really sunk, wasn't he? He was up late, eating sugary treats (he'd sampled more than his fair share) and consuming caffeine—three things that were very much against Athena's rigid dietary rules as well as his rehab training plan. And despite his love for his career, and his desire to return to the ice still in his prime, he found that in this moment, he would follow wherever Jenny led him.

* * *

Giggling, Jenny leaned against Dylan's shoulder. He was hopeless with the piping bag. He'd over-flooded one of his cookies and the runnier icing had breached the thicker icing's ringed barrier. He was cursing under his breath, his competitive streak coming out as he tried to stop the icing from spilling off his cookie.

She hadn't had this much fun in ages—at least since their

tavern date, and before that, Thanksgiving. Maybe she didn't need grand adventures. Maybe she just needed someone like Dylan in her life. Someone who made the everyday *feel* like an adventure.

Sometimes, she even forgot that his hockey life existed. The fame, the fortune, the articles about his injury and speculation about a trade. None of it seemed real. He was just a regular guy she really enjoyed hanging out with.

Dylan kept glancing at her cookies, then back at his own. Quite frankly, she had a feeling Rylnn could do better than Dylan currently was.

"I like how you're mixing the colors," she said. She loved the fact that a man who was at the pinnacle of professional hockey was struggling with something she found easy.

"Liar." He picked up the cookie he'd been working on, glared at her, then popped the whole thing into his mouth. He closed his eyes, scrunching his face as he chewed, complaining, "So much sugar."

"But it tastes so delicious, doesn't it?"

He allowed one eye to open into a slit as he continued to glare. "You're a horrible influence. I'll bet you're doing this so you can hold it over my head with Athena."

She grinned. "Thanks for the idea!"

"When I get kicked off the team and end up homeless, I'm gonna come sleep on your couch."

"Good. I could use some help around here." She piped some blue icing over pink, then dragged a toothpick through the colors, creating a pink-and-blue design.

She stepped back, looking at the rows of cookies. Things had definitely gotten out of hand with the number of cookies they'd baked, but they were beautiful. Well, for the most part. Some were a complete disaster. But if you closed your eyes, they all tasted the same—a theory Dylan seemed intent on testing thoroughly.

"So my recipe wins," he announced. He swept his palm across the counter, smearing wet icing and gathering errant sprinkles. He dropped them into his free hand before dusting them into the trash.

"Since when did we decide on that?"

"I've seen you eating lots of cookies. Mine."

"Yours are different. That's all."

"They're delicious."

"Mine are better. Prettier."

"I had no idea you were such a liar."

"Mine are better," she insisted.

Truthfully, his were the best. There was something decadent about the texture. They were slightly softer and melted in her mouth more than her own did. With less icing and sprinkles, she noticed the wonderful blend of sugar, butter and flour. They were perfect, but she'd never admit it.

Dylan glowered down at her, his mouth set at a stern angle. And yet, it lacked an edge, proving to her that it was nothing but an act.

"Tell me the truth or you'll regret it," he growled.

She pretended to think about it, eyes raised upward, curious to see what he'd do if she denied him the gratification of winning their cookie contest. "Let me think... Nope. Can't go with regret."

"You have two seconds to change your mind."

"Don't need them."

"That's it." His arms snaked out, his fingers dancing up her sides.

She squirmed and let out a shriek as he tackled her, holding her close when she bent to the side in an attempt to escape. A cackle broke free and he shushed her so she wouldn't wake up Gramps.

"Unfair!" she gasped as he tickled her, his pursuit unrelenting. Despite having his foot in a cast, he seemed to predict her every move, keeping her trapped as his fingers continued to dance across her skin.

She crashed into him, helpless with laughter.

The tickling ceased and his arms locked around her. With his mouth over her ear, he whispered, "Admit the truth, you evil woman."

"No way."

His arms unlocked, his fingers finding their way to her most sensitive, ticklish spots. She tumbled to the floor, but he followed, his body pressed over hers. She gasped as helpless, silent laughter sent her stomach into aching spasms.

"Mercy! Mercy! I give up."

His fingers halted, his body a warm weight against hers. "Say it."

"My cookies are better."

Her shirt had come untucked during their shenanigans, and the next hit of tickles landed against bare skin. She inhaled at the contact and his hand flattened as it slid up her side, no longer dancing.

Her breath came out in pants and Dylan froze on top of her, the tickle war forgotten. Impatiently, she fisted his shirt and yanked him to her. They kissed until dawn slowly sent fingers of sunlight into the room and a distant rooster crowed.

For a long time, he stayed on the floor beside her, propped on one hip, his body leaning against hers, his hand tracing idle circles on her stomach. He placed a tender kiss against her cheek, releasing a small groan of approval as though kissing her cheek was the most erotic thing he'd encountered.

She aimed his face toward her own, kissing him again, her lips swollen, her body spent. It had been a long time since she had stayed up all night, laughing and making out.

"I should go," he murmured, stealing another kiss before reluctantly sitting up.

She sat up as well, adjusting her shirt. "I look forward to the day you have to start living on my couch because you've been kicked off the team for eating too many of my delicious cookies."

His brows lowered over stormy eyes.

"My couch is much closer than San Antonio," she said sweetly as he took her hand to help her up. He stood, pulling her to her feet as though she weighed nothing.

He pulled her close for another kiss. "At this rate I'll be on your couch within the week."

"I think I can make that timeline work."

"And what would your grandfather think?" he asked.

She automatically glanced toward the hallway that led to the bedrooms. It was a miracle they hadn't woken him with all of their laughing and banging around.

"I'm sure he'd understand," she whispered, longing to tuck her body against Dylan's again, to hear his heartbeat, feel his solid warmth. Any excuse to keep him a moment longer, to prevent this unexpected night from ending.

He stepped closer as though he'd read her mind, fitting his body around hers and giving her one last kiss, sealing their date as possibly her favorite one so far.

CHAPTER 7

On Monday, Jenny snuck out of her shop, leaving April in charge. She desperately needed a dose of caffeine to make her feel human again after staying up all night. In a few months, once April was on maternity leave, Jenny would have to flip the "Back in Five" sign and lock up if she needed to sneak out for a few minutes.

With luck, April would be able to work right up to her due date in early March, just a few days after Jenny's own late February birthday. The idea of hiring someone to replace April temporarily felt like more bother than it would be worth, but she supposed if she wanted to have a life, she'd better find someone.

Jenny took a few steps up the street and slipped into the Longhorn Diner. The scents of the fryer, garlic and butter hit her and she inhaled deeply, waiting for the hint of coffee to reach her. Ah, there it was. She needed some of that in her.

She made her way to the back of the diner, taking in the Christmas lights framing the window between the server's prep area and the cook. There was just a little over two weeks before Christmas. Should she get a gift for Dylan? They'd only had three dates…

She sat on one of the red stools at the back counter, her chin propped on her hand. Mrs. Fisher was busy waiting on a table and Jenny debated helping herself to a cup of coffee. However, she'd heard the scolding Levi Wylder got when he decided to help himself, and it didn't seem worth it.

Her phone vibrated with a text, and Jenny pulled it from her back pocket to take a peek. *Dylan.* No matter how tired she was, the man made her smile. He'd sent her the image of a wet and cranky looking cat in front of a cup of coffee.

The next text said *I feel like this cat.*

She smiled and typed back, *Me too.* Then she sent a picture of the diner's coffeepot which was a few feet away, waiting for Mrs. Fisher. *So close and yet so far.* She added, *Try to nap on the plane.* This afternoon he was en route to the team's away game, and apparently making good use of the plane's WiFi by messaging back and forth with her—the perfect thing to help her forget her fatigue.

Bubbles appeared on the screen, showing that Dylan was typing a reply, and she set her phone down as the waitress, Mrs. Fisher, drew near.

"Inventory season already?" the woman asked, the coffeepot she was carrying sadly empty. She slid it onto the machine's burner and grabbed the full pot, then turned back to Jenny. "You look like you've been up all night."

"I was."

Mrs. Fisher poured a cup for Jenny, and she inhaled the sweet scent of salvation. *Coffee.* Jenny guzzled the black liquid before gasping at its heat.

Mrs. Fisher watched, unimpressed. "You need to get a pot for your shop, hon. By the time you come in here, you're desperate."

"I'm trying to cut down," she said, mincing her words so she could blow on her cup.

"You say that every day." Mrs. Fisher set down two creams beside the sugar bowl.

Jenny doctored her drink and took a slower, more cautious sip. Much better. She was feeling more human already.

Something flashed in Mrs. Fisher's teased-up, bleached hair and Jenny squinted at her. "What's in your hair?"

The woman smiled and patted her do. "Christmas lights." She turned her head so Jenny could see it better.

"Amazing."

The woman studied her. "You have that pinched look, like you forgot to eat." Mrs. Fisher clucked and shook her head.

"Maybe. I ate a lot of cookies last night." She yawned. "Or maybe that was this morning." She waited for the woman to pump her for gossip about why she'd lost track of time.

"A woman your age needs sleep, not a sugar rush, hon."

"Maybe someone was keeping me up."

"Mmhm." Mrs. Fisher set about making a fresh pot of coffee to replace the one she'd emptied.

"One of the Dragons."

"I never got into fantasy novels," the woman said absently.

"No, a—never mind."

When she was younger, and dragging her butt into the diner looking for coffee because she'd been up too late, everyone had assumed it was because of a man. Why didn't anyone make that assumption now? She'd hinted around with April about last night when her assistant had come in a few hours ago, later than usual because of a scheduled ultrasound. But her pregnant friend had been too busy, going on about how it looked like she was going to have a girl this time, to pick up the hints.

Jenny was happy for April, but she kind of wanted to spill the beans about her own adventures. Maybe if she could find Daisy-Mae, the two of them could indulge in a little girl-talk. Or even Miranda, the team's owner, would do. She'd bought a little place outside of town and was often kicking about when she wasn't in the city working. She just had to tell *someone*!

"Did you have lunch?" Mrs. Fisher asked, her face showing concern.

Jenny straightened, blinking at the time on her phone's locked screen. She squinted at the glass. It looked like it was almost three in the afternoon.

She shook her head and checked the clock behind Mrs. Fisher. Yup. It was three already. The store had received the first spring shipment, even though it was still only December. Prepping the new stock while texting with Dylan had kept her busy all morning, and apparently, most of the afternoon as well.

Trying to find space for the new items had been a challenge. She really needed to get those renovations finished up so she could move stock into the new room.

"Pie?" Mrs. Fisher asked, already lifting the glass lid from her displayed apple pie—one of her favorites. She should pack a slice up for Gramps for dessert tonight, even though they had plenty of cookies.

"I shouldn't." Jenny patted her middle, staring at the flaky-crusted pie. She felt a bit off, thanks to all of the sugar from last night.

"Don't be like that. You're gorgeous."

"You sound like Dylan."

"If you want pie, you have pie. It's that simple."

"I love you."

The woman smiled knowingly and slid a slice of apple pie in front of Jenny. "Eat your dessert first; life's uncertain, hon." Then she was off to peddle her desserts to more softies who lacked self-restraint. Mrs. Fisher was one of the many reasons Jenny loved this diner so much.

While she ate, she checked her phone, knowing there'd be a reply from Dylan.

Already napped. Got half a moustache drawn on me by Mullens. What I wouldn't give to have him traded. What are you doing tonight?

She was tempted to reply with a sassy comment, but instead set down her phone. Her friends would surely tell her to wait, and not appear too eager, as if she was sitting around, waiting for him to text her.

Screw it. She picked up her phone. If she wanted pie, she was having pie. If she wanted to message a hottie hockey player, she was going to.

When do you get home?

Early tomorrow morning.

So you're just being nosy asking what I'm up to? Worried there's another man?

She saw three dots appear, then disappear. Had she gone too far?

She sighed and put down her phone. Then she picked it up again and whipped out another message. *I bet you wish there was an emoji for grunting. Then you could grunt your replies.*

Oh boy, she was really pushing it now. But when they were chatting in real life, he'd often use body language or small sounds to suffice as a reply. Texting was likely difficult for the man.

He sent a grumpy face emoji and she laughed.

Learning how to read his moods was like learning a secret language.

Tomorrow night then? What are you up to? she texted.

Getting my cast off and then sleeping on your grandfather's couch. Think he'll mind?

She bit back her smile. *Didn't take you long to get fired. Did they give you a second lecture along with a pink slip?*

He'd revealed earlier in the day that he'd gotten an earful for showing up at work exhausted. She was a little fuzzy on exactly what he did at the rink with his foot in a cast, but it seemed as though hockey still took up a lot of time with workouts, training, workshops and, of course, games.

Still employed he replied.

Disappointing. You'll have to do something about that. This small town isn't quite as exciting without you in it.

She inhaled as she hit send. There was no beating around the bush with that reply. She liked him. But she supposed he already knew that.

No shotguns or armadillos today? he asked.

Nope. No power outages, cookie bake-offs, or escaped chickens, either. Just adding new inventory and trying to stay awake. Hey, when's your birthday? An idea for a gag gift was coming to mind.

February 26.

Shut up.

The dots appeared, then disappeared.

That's my birthday, too! she revealed.

We'll have to celebrate together.

She smiled at the idea, hoping he'd still be in Texas at the end of February. But if he wasn't, maybe she could take a quick trip to wherever he was and hang out with him for the day.

Deal. But I choose the cake. You might pick something without icing and sprinkles.

You're literally trying to kill me, aren't you? Or at least get me kicked off the team.

Giggling to herself, Jenny glanced around the diner, then surreptitiously licked a finger and dabbed the flakes of pastry crumbs resting on her plate. She dropped them in her mouth just as Mrs. Fisher slid an individual sized pie in front of her. It looked like chicken pot pie, but smelled and looked a bit different. Slightly sketchy, in fact.

"Try this," Mrs. Fisher said. "It's new."

"What is it?" Jenny sampled a bite while the woman watched.

"Like it?"

It was salmon. Salmon pie.

Was she going to have to politely eat this? Pay for it? She came to the diner so she got stuff she *did* want to eat.

"Sure." Jenny eyed the pie. Maybe she could ask to have it boxed to go and feed it to her cat.

"You don't like it."

"I'm not much of a seafood person."

"You have fish and chips all the time."

"That's different."

"Fish and chips is seafood, hon. And this is a healthier option for you and your grandfather. Has he had his cholesterol checked lately?"

Jenny grumbled a reply. Mrs. Fisher didn't get it. Fish and chips was special. It was on the hidden side of the food pyramid. It was over with other important foods like chocolate and coffee. The *dark* side. Fish and chips were the other, *other* white meat. Salmon was very firmly in the seafood category on the proper side of the pyramid.

Daisy-Mae slid onto the stool beside Jenny, bringing with her the scent of expensive hand lotion. She leaned over Jenny's pie with a frown. "What's that?"

"Mrs. Fisher is mothering me. She's making me eat salmon."

"It's for your health," the older woman called. "And I'm sending a salad for Garfield next time you order him lunch."

There was no way her grandfather would eat the leafy greens, but there was no use arguing with Mrs. Fisher. Plus, she admitted their diet had gotten a tad out of hand lately. When her parents returned for the holidays, they'd surely comment on it. Maybe it was time to work a few more vegetables into their week.

"So?" Daisy-Mae asked Jenny after ordering a cup of coffee to go. "Did Dylan ever call you?"

"Yeah." Jenny checked the diner's clock. "Hey, aren't you supposed to be working in the city right now?"

"I worked from home today." She drummed her long nails on the countertop. "So?"

This was her chance to talk about Dylan. But she was suddenly shy. "Umm…what's it like dating Maverick—like the hockey and NHL part?"

Daisy-Mae thanked Mrs. Fisher for the coffee, then stood, turning to face Jenny. "There's just one thing you have to remember: Hockey comes first. Always. The second thing is… the press is sneaky. If you two stop fighting and decide to date—"

"We're not fighting."

"Mav says you hate each other."

"We don't hate each other." She felt her face flush with heat.

"Well, if you ever become an item with a Dragon, watch out for reporters." She slung her designer handbag over her shoulder. "I thought I was used to attention because of all the beauty pageants I've been in." She shook her head. "This is way different. Small towns protect us, but when you're with someone well-known, you wise up real fast to what the rest of the world is like."

She shot Jenny a wan, slightly lovesick smile. "Then again, some men are worth it." She gave Jenny's elbow a squeeze and left.

So this time that Jenny was spending with Dylan was just a beautiful small town bubble?

And why did Maverick still think she and Dylan disliked each other?

Then again, not being badgered about their relationship and where it was going, while unusual, was also nice. The people of Sweetheart Creek had a way of putting their noses into everyone else's business. When she'd dated Ranger, the townspeople had expected to hear wedding bells any moment, and it had gone to her head. It hadn't taken them long to convince her they were right when, truthfully, there'd been signs all along that her relationship with Ranger wasn't going to make the distance.

Jenny picked up her phone again, processing her friend's words.

She was treading in girlfriend territory with Dylan now, meaning she might be photographed with him. Would social media comments be kind? Would someone come out and say that she should shed some weight if she wanted to keep Dylan?

She inhaled sharply, stopping her thoughts in their tracks.

Happy bubble. She was in a happy bubble with a hottie. She checked her phone again.

Dylan had texted back *What time tomorrow night?*

She felt the smile stretch across her face. Who needed sleep? She was going to spend the evening with her hockey hottie tomorrow. *Seven? I have to run some errands after work.*

You leaving me out of Secret Santa?

This one's for my four-legged friends.

Need supplies from the city?

He was going to be sorry he'd asked. She fired off the rescue shelter's lengthy wish list, curious to see if, like before, Dylan would check off every item. It was unlikely, given the amount. But a girl never knew with a guy like Dylan.

* * *

Dylan could hardly keep his eyes open despite having hit the Snooze button on his alarm clock several times that morning. A late Sunday night with Jenny, followed by a late Monday night at an away game, and he was toast today. And, like a teenager who cared little about consequences, he was planning another night out in Sweetheart Creek with Jenny again.

He checked his phone for a text from her, but there was nothing new. Yesterday they'd texted up a storm, but today they were both a bit quieter, having to actually apply themselves at work again.

Athena Gavras, the team's dietician, had already busted him for not listening twice in her pre-Christmas dietary lecture, even though the holiday was still almost two weeks away.

He propped his chin on a fist, leaning on the conference

room table for support. His eyes drifted shut and he snapped them awake, forcing himself to focus on Athena. Maybe he could sneak a nap while Karlene, the team's physical therapist, worked on his foot after this meeting. Although, that was an unlikely dream. She'd probably be putting him through his paces, since the team doctor had taken another x-ray this morning and had left his cast off afterward. It felt good to be able to move his right foot and ankle again. He almost moaned in joy when he kicked off his shoe, gently rolling his ankle and arching his stiff and achy foot under the table. He'd thought that cast was never going to come off.

There would be no nap. Then again, if Karlene worked him hard enough, it might wake him up.

Athena listed a few tips and tricks on how to prevent blowing up her diet plans over the upcoming Christmas break —typical stuff like how to avoid sugar, and what to fill up on so they didn't binge on cookies.

He winced, thinking about how he'd blown right past her rules the night before last. He would never admit it, but Jenny's cookies, loaded with icing, were addictive. Not as good as his recipe, but they filled an inexplicable hole inside him. Kind of like his addiction to Jenny. It made no sense.

"Dylan?" Athena asked. "You had a question?"

"Sorry?" His head had slipped off his propped-up arm, making it look as though he'd raised his hand to ask something. "Right. Just wanted to say thanks. Good reminders."

"Suck up," Leo muttered, leaning back in his chair, thumbs hooked behind his large belt buckle—no doubt a rodeo win.

Mullens, however, smirked. For some weird reason, the guy had decided that Athena was his enemy from day one on the team. Maybe Santa would bring Mullens a better attitude when it came to the team's dietician.

"Thank you, Dylan." She looked pleased, a smile warming her face.

After Athena was done, Miranda Fairchild, the team's owner, and Dak Morisette, head of the Dragons' charity as well as Miranda's new boyfriend, took to the front of the room to talk about the upcoming gala. Dylan didn't plan on going, but he thought some of the silent auction items might make good Christmas gifts for Jenny.

When the meetings were over, Athena caught up with him, her dark brown wavy hair bouncing. "When you're back on the ice next month, your calorie consumption's going to need to increase again. If you want some new recipes or tips to beat the monster in your stomach, let me know."

"Thanks." He nodded, knowing how she must feel sometimes—like an outsider. He made a point of looking her in the eye. "I appreciate it."

She blushed, and he couldn't help wondering what a sweetheart like her was doing dealing with a bunch of jerky jocks all day. He knew she was opening a bookstore across from Jenny's boutique soon and he hoped she wasn't planning to stop working with him and his teammates. Even though Mullens acted like she was a nag, she was really good at her job and he'd learned a lot from her, despite decades of careful diet planning.

Dylan cut left in the hallway, wishing he was heading to Sweetheart Creek ahead of schedule and not Karlene's chamber of pain. Because, even as tired as he was, there was only one place he wanted to be right now, and it wasn't in the team's physical therapy room talking about his foot.

He scowled when he saw a small herd of reporters being escorted down the halls by the captain's girlfriend, Daisy-Mae.

"Sorry," she said to Dylan, turning to walk backward in her black stilettos as if she was born in them, keeping her long-lashed eyes on the reporters. "Follow me, follow me."

"What's this?" Dylan's teammate Landon asked, stopping beside him to let the group go by.

"An advance sneak peek at new merchandise," one said, waving a pass in front of Dylan's face and snapping a close-up.

"Get lost," Dylan grumbled.

"Care to comment on your foot, Dylan?" the reporter asked, eyeing his newly cast-free right foot.

Dylan gently pointed a camera down, wishing he could crush the thing.

"I heard you're transitioning into active recovery. Does that mean a full recovery? Do you have a comment on when you'll return to play?"

Landon grinned at Dylan, happily past the injury and rehab phase with his own ankle injury and the never-ending questions that opened the gaping hell of self-doubts and what-ifs. Landon had healed and moved on with his life and career. He had a daughter—Rylnn—and looked as though he was crushing on his nanny, Cassandra. To Dylan, Landon was taking advantage of one of life's pleasant upswings.

Dylan, however, wasn't sure he was on one at the moment and he glared at the reporter, not caring that he'd be labeled a grump in the papers. He didn't need to be popular like his teammates. The only thing he needed was the love of one good woman.

And he had a pretty good feeling he'd found her.

* * *

Dylan sat on the massage table, pointing the toes on his right foot like a ballerina. It was a relief to be out of the cast, but it was stiffer than he'd anticipated, even after being wrapped in heat and slowly stretched out by the expert standing beside him.

"Any pain?" Karlene, the team's physical therapist, asked as she finished working his arch.

Of course there was. And his foot was also aching from the forty-five minutes of prodding and exercises she'd put him through.

He shook his head and checked his watch. "Not bad." He'd planned to be on the road by now. Jenny wouldn't be waiting yet, but he wanted to optimize the amount of time they had for their stay-at-home movie date after running errands together. He'd even worn a soft sweater that he hoped enticed Jenny to cuddle up to him. Although, he expected her grandfather would be home, which might put a damper on that.

Karlene picked up her tablet which contained her digital archive of player records from injuries and recovery plans, as well as who knew what else. She'd already performed a miracle earlier in the season by getting Landon back on the ice. The man had pretty much shattered his ankle and she'd managed to get him back on skates. Now, Landon could pop up and down in the net like his ankle had never been operated on. But that was Landon. What if the woman was fresh out of miracles and this was as good as his foot would get?

"What's that?" Dylan asked, pointing to the diamond on Karlene's left hand. It wasn't huge, but it was definitely an engagement ring.

"You need an eye test."

"What? I have 20-20." He covered one eye, then the other,

peering at the recovery workout posters across the room. Sharp and crisp, like always.

"I've been engaged for months, Dylan."

In other words, he'd seen her dozens of times, but had never noticed. And, judging by her expression, the thrill of talking about her upcoming nuptials had already worn off.

"When's the big day?"

She inhaled and exhaled in a way that reminded him of mothers shopping with toddlers in grocery stores. "Soon." She rubbed her forehead. "Sorry, it's just a lot. The idea of getting married is overwhelming. And it's a short engagement which means all the prep is ramped up. Not that anyone's letting me get involved in it." She gave a weak smile that wasn't at all like the ones Jenny beamed his way. There was no sunshine on Karlene's weather radar today. "You know. Church. Dress. Wedding party. Invites. Color schemes. The whole deal. And when you throw all the usual Christmas stuff on top of it all…" She sighed again.

Wow. She made it all sound…awful. Personally, though, he'd never imagined the work that went into a wedding. His focus was more on the day when he'd have someone to come home to.

"Shotgun wedding?" he asked, his mind immediately going to Mrs. Filmore and her realistic shotgun audio track. The woman had scared the pants off him—not that he'd ever admit it to anyone.

Karlene scoffed, her eyes rolling like a teenager's. "Check the century, Dylan. And no."

Okay, maybe not a shotgun wedding, but even he could tell there was something off. It was more than the stress of finding a church and the right dress. Maybe it was the groom. Maybe she was falling into marriage with a high school sweetheart she'd never gotten around to dumping. She had a vein of loyalty that he figured could cause her problems. Although going as far as marrying someone because of loyalty seemed extreme.

That was another thing he loved about Jenny. She was loyal, but not about to bow to anyone else's wishes. Not even his own. And yet she'd drop everything for her family or community. He had a feeling her Secret Santa acts stretched her financially, but she'd never let on about it. It had felt good to have the resources to step up and help.

"I'm clearing you for light practice as part of your active recovery plan. But don't overdo it," Karlene announced, her tone stern. "And come to me if you experience anything abnormal. Pain. Swelling. Fatigue."

"So you don't want to talk wedding flowers, color schemes and menus?"

She frowned at him, a deep line between her brows. "Are you…kidding around?" She placed a hand over his forehead and he tried to lean away. "You feeling okay?"

He gave a half shrug, well aware that he didn't have a history of cracking jokes. "Just happy to be on the ice again."

Which was true. He had a lot of work to do, though. Despite doing all the workouts he'd been able to with one foot in a cast, he knew he was deconditioned and that if he didn't work hard, his fitness numbers at this year's summer training camp would be significantly lower than last year's. And that would negatively impact contract negotiations for the next year.

Work hard. Get traded up. That had always been the plan.

Right now, though, he wasn't sure if it was just the mountain of effort he saw in front of him, or if he was simply tired of being traded. The idea of facing yet another move—even if it would take him back to a city and a team he already knew—was demoralizing. He'd only hung out with Jenny a few times, but he could see a future that involved her, Sweetheart Creek *and* hockey. And that meant staying put and not getting traded back to Denver. Or anywhere else, for that matter.

Karlene grabbed her tablet again, her ring winking under the lights as she tapped and scrolled. He wondered if there was a pool among the guys about her engagement. Namely, about how long the marriage would last. There probably wasn't because generally guys didn't tend to notice those sorts of things, even though he knew they'd have no qualms about betting on it.

The door to Karlene's room of torture opened and Miranda, the team's owner, popped her head in. She spotted Dylan and smiled, then strode in, her black hair wound into a high bun.

"I heard today is the big day!" Miranda stopped beside Dylan, eyeing his foot. "How's it feel?"

He nodded and flexed his foot for her. "All right."

"If all goes well," Karlene said, "he'll be cleared for games by mid to late January as planned."

"Good," Miranda stated.

Dylan sat a bit straighter, hoping again that he'd more than earn back the big dollars Miranda had poured into his career. He'd heard she'd used her own money to start and build the team, something her family—as well as anyone else with an opinion—had been against. He'd like to think he was worth his keep.

As though reading his earlier thoughts, or possibly addressing a few of Miranda's previous concerns, Karlene added, "I don't think this injury, with Dylan's work ethic, will hold him back or negatively impact negotiations."

"Denver's dying to know how you're doing," Miranda said.

Dylan nodded, aware that they wanted insider info, straight from the horse's mouth, about how he was healing before digging further into preliminary trade negotiations. He'd had the odd call from his old team's management as well as his former teammate Darian, who had nothing positive to say about how his own season was going without Dylan there as backup. The calls had increased to the point he'd started ignoring his phone unless it sang a Carrie Underwood song—his ringtone for Jenny. By association, he was almost starting to like the country singer's music.

Karlene winked at Dylan. "Well, with any kind of luck, we won't get stuck with your sorry self for an extra season."

Miranda laughed, a good sport about the fact that her team hadn't experienced the best start in the NHL despite her efforts to line them up for success, and that many of her players were hoping to score a trade to a different team. However, that might soon change now that the Dragons were finally pulling together and winning a few games.

But that wasn't the main reason the idea of staying with the Dragons for another year held a lot more appeal for Dylan than it had a month ago.

At the moment, staying put meant being with Jenny.

Although, if he *was* traded, maybe she'd come on the road with him. She wanted to travel and her goofy sense of adventure would make everything fun. He could imagine what it would be like if he could convince Jenny to leave the store in April's hands after she had her baby. He and Jenny could go off and explore new cities every time he had an away game. New restaurants, playing tourist, taking in the local entertainment.

"Okay, I'm going to head to the media room. There's a

press conference in ten." Miranda double-checked her smart watch, then addressed Dylan. "You still prefer I be the one to update everyone about your foot?"

He nodded. "Thanks." It was too early for him to know anything for certain, and he didn't want to cause any speculation. Miranda was the expert, and he was more than happy to leave the press to her, and avoid giving the reporters anything they could use to twist him into someone he wasn't in order to sell their articles. He'd learned that when he got twisted around enough times, he often lost sense of who he truly was.

"He's cleared for light practice?" Miranda confirmed with Karlene.

"You bet."

"Good work, you two," Miranda said with a warm smile before leaving the room.

Karlene used a gold stylus to scrawl something on her matching tablet, then handed it all to Dylan. "Sign and I'll send it up to management for filing."

He held the digital pen over the signature line, letting the words floating in front of him sink in. Cleared for light practice.

Soon it would say cleared to return to play. Return to play.

He inhaled, allowing the idea to settle through him like the warmth from Karlene's therapeutic heat lamp. Deeper and deeper.

It felt unreal, being back on the ice, in the center of things. Soon he'd be back to angling for more game time and better contracts.

"What's wrong?" Karlene asked, her ring flashing again. Jenny would like that ring, but the center stone wasn't quite right. What was it? The shape? Color? No, it was too big. That was what it was. Jenny didn't love drawing attention to herself.

"Hello?" Karlene had bent over in an attempt to make eye contact with him, her blond and brown hair tumbling off her shoulders.

"Hm?" He looked up, his thoughts falling away.

"It's not unusual for an older player such as yourself to have concerns about returning to play and the long-term impact of their time off-ice."

He scowled at the age reference and added his signature to the digital document. He handed the tech back to Karlene and she hugged it to her chest while he stood.

"Any plans for Christmas?" she asked, as he slowly eased his weight onto both feet, waiting to see if there'd be a slice of pain. There wasn't.

He nodded.

"Netherlands?"

He grunted a yes.

"Long flight. You only have three days off. Don't come back wiped out. We have a lot of work to do."

"Won't you be on your honeymoon?"

"That's not until the end of season and after calving is done."

She was marrying a rancher. Somehow that fit.

He frowned as his bodyweight stretched his arch. It was uncomfortable but not bad. The real problem, though, was that it was two weeks before Christmas and he had a flurry of games that week, plus his trip away. There was going to be a stretch of at least five to six days in a row where it would be impossible for him and Jenny to hang out. And shortly after that, he'd be working up to game play again. Trade talks would amp up in at least a month from now, and he could be gone from San Antonio before he was ready. If he ever was.

"You okay?" Karlene was giving him a worried look. "Foot hurt?"

Her hand was on his arm, ready to manhandle him back onto the bed should he nod. He waved her off. His foot wasn't the problem. Finding a way to spend more time with Jenny before hockey whisked him away? That was definitely a problem.

CHAPTER 8

Jenny led Dylan into the back of Call of the Wyld(er), Brant Wylder's veterinary clinic in Sweetheart Creek. It was also the temporary home of the local animal shelter, and the destination for Jenny's pre-date errands and Dylan's long list of purchased pet supplies.

The two had met up at Blue Tumbleweed, Dylan standing mute for a moment in the store's doorway, his gaze traveling over her new navy wool dress, jean jacket and worn boots. She'd felt self-conscious until she caught the glint of hunger in his eyes. He strode over to her, his speed much faster now that he was no longer hindered by a cast, and swept her into his arms for a hello kiss.

Not a bad way to start an evening.

The agony she'd endured picking the right outfit had been well worth it.

As they walked further into the clinic with their armloads of kibble, the scent of antiseptic filled Jenny's nostrils. A green parrot greeted them from its wooden perch as they headed toward the storage room. "Don't be a stranger!"

"How do you do?" Dylan chirped back.

"How do you do? How do you do?" repeated the parrot, causing Dylan to chuckle.

"Hey." Brant, April's husband and the owner of the vet clinic and local animal rescue, came hustling from an exam room, his cowboy boots clacking on the shiny floor, a squirming cat in his arms. "Thanks. Just put it wherever you can find space."

He situated the cat in a kennel and quickly closed the door, then joined Jenny and Dylan in the storeroom.

"Here." He grabbed a bag from Jenny and tossed it on a short pile of food near the floor.

"You're mixing cat and dog food," Jenny protested.

"Robyn will organize it for me later."

"Or we could do it now," Jenny said, shifting a bag from one pile to another.

Dylan set down his bags and Jenny admired the way his body moved under his black, gold and green Dragons jacket. He was such a tasty athlete.

"There's more," Jenny said proudly, her heart expanding at how Dylan had bought everything she'd put on the list, along with a small furry toy for her own cat, Fifty.

They headed back to the alley where the SUV Dylan had borrowed for the errand was waiting to be unloaded.

"Spoiler alert," Jenny said, tossing a box of treats, leashes, and collars to Brant. "Dylan's your Secret Santa. He finished off your wish list, and you didn't even have to sit on his lap."

Brant chuckled and shook his head at the filled car. "I don't know what to say. Thank you. Thank you so much." He shook Dylan's hand.

Dylan bashfully scratched his forehead, shrugging off Brant's comment. Then a flash of black fur hit him in the side of the leg, knocking him off balance as a large dog leaped into the back of the car. It squeezed between the bags of food and the window, then promptly sat and grinned at Dylan.

Brant gave an embarrassed laugh. "Sorry." He slapped his thigh. "Come on, Fish."

The dog hesitated, clearly not wanting to miss out on a car ride. Brant stepped forward, taking it by the collar. "She's our latest rescue. She freaks out whenever we put her in a kennel and chews on the bars until her gums bleed or she chips her teeth. So, we let her roam."

"Aw. Poor thing." Jenny reached over and ruffled the dog's ears. The dog smiled up at Jenny, tail wagging.

"She's very social. She thinks everyone should be her friend and she'll sit with dogs or cats who are hurt or sick. She's really empathetic and surprisingly gentle—even though she has no clue how enormous she is or that not everyone wants to be besties."

Jenny could see Brant eyeing Dylan as he spoke, no doubt sizing up whether the dog and hockey player would be a match. Brant was jokingly referred to as a furry friend match-maker—he'd set up almost everyone in town with a homeless cat or dog.

"She reminds me of the dog we had as a kid," Dylan said, the edges of his mouth lifting just enough to show how much he'd loved the four-legged friend. He crouched and Fish waggled her way over, dragging Brant, who still had her by the collar. He released her and the dog flopped in front of Dylan, belly to the sky.

Dylan scratched Fish's shaggy stomach. "Jenny says you're building a shelter?" he said to Brant.

"We're working on it," Brant grumbled, "But Cassandra bought the Peppermint Lodge so that building's out."

"Let it go," Jenny teased, well aware that her friend—Rylnn's nanny—had big plans to turn the old hunting lodge into a wedding venue.

Brant led the dog back inside while Dylan and Jenny brought in another load. Fish obeyed, but not before giving Dylan a soulful gaze which was echoed right back.

"You look smitten," Jenny said, nudging him.

"I miss having a dog."

"I guess it's hard when you're away so much?"

"Yeah, but I could probably make it work."

They dropped off the supplies and managed to leave the dog, Fish, behind despite a wistful backward glance from Dylan. Next they headed over to Jenny's for their movie date.

Jenny let them in, calling out to Gramps, "We're home!"

There was no answer, but she found a note on the counter.

"He says Maria took him to Bingo." Jenny grinned at Dylan. They had the place to themselves. "Let me introduce you to the couch."

They headed into the living room, and Jenny waved at the plain gray piece across from the fireplace and TV. The couch, one of the few pieces of furniture she'd brought with her when she'd moved in, was long and lower to the ground than most. It was also completely out of sync with the charming old country house. Along one pale green wall was a stone fireplace, and the room had thick plank floors and wide wood trim around every wooden door. Gramps' armchair, which was a giant, overstuffed brown number, fit with the room better than her couch, but she hadn't wanted to let it go.

"I know she doesn't quite work with the room."

"She?" Dylan asked.

"Yes. She's the wrong tone, her legs are too skinny, and her cushions are too square, but I love her." Jenny flopped onto the couch with a satisfied sigh. "Especially with all of these." She flung her arms out into the bright array of throw cushions that had half-buried her when she'd landed. "Gramps hates her."

Dylan sank down beside Jenny, as if it was the first time he'd had a chance to sit all day. He let out a sigh of satisfaction, then frowned, wiggling his torso as though trying to get comfy.

"She's firm, I know." Jenny bent one leg under her, smoothing out the skirt of her dress. She readjusted the opera-length string of beads around her neck and tucked a large throw pillow under her arm, leaning toward him. "But isn't it great? Support below…"—she patted the firm couch—"and then all of these lovely soft cushions to cozy up in."

"Women are strange."

She sat up, gave an indignant gasp, then smacked him with one of the cushions. But his reflexes were fast. His hand snatched the turquoise fabric and before she knew it, it was brushing up the side of her face, messing up her hair.

"You didn't!" Not caring that she was wearing a dress and trying to do the casually sexy thing, she leapt to her feet, snatching a pillow in each hand and swinging them toward his head.

He laughed, the sound incredible. It was deep, smooth and like a balm. He ducked, his arms snaking around her waist, pulling her onto the couch beside him. He was strong, moving her as if her weight was insubstantial, his body pinning her.

She grabbed another cushion, but he knocked it from her hand, then the rest onto the floor where they slid out of reach.

"No fair!"

"Very fair." He settled alongside her, his gaze taking her in with a sweep. "I like your dress. Did I tell you that?" He ran a hand up the side of her dress's fitted bodice as though he had all the time in the world.

She squirmed, reaching down to make sure the asymmetrical skirt hadn't flipped too high during their antics. "Thanks."

"Is it for me?" His hand ran down her side at that same leisurely pace, cupping the curve of her hip.

"The dress? Don't flatter yourself." Of course it was for him. She'd spent an hour working her way through the racks in her store, finally deciding to try the wool dress. The material hugged her chest, then flowed over the rest of her body, hitting just below the knee. She'd paired it with a jean jacket and boots to give her a more casual look, and had left her hair down for once.

His lips twitched. He knew she'd dressed up for him.

She was going to tell him not to get used to it, but he lowered his lips to hers. Soon she was lost exploring his mouth, his reactions, and the way his hand steadily caressed her while his lips moved. She felt special, wanted, needed. As if he got the same pleasure as she did from that delicious little tug of her hair that sent a riot of fireworks and shivers through her nervous system.

She deepened the kiss, her hands exploring his back, the tight muscles, the way they moved and flexed based on his own explorations. They fell into sync, tasting and nipping.

"No other woman has ever kissed me," Dylan whispered when they broke apart to catch their breath. He rested a finger lightly over her lips, gently tracing the sensitive flesh when she went to argue. There was no way their kisses were his first. Not a man like him.

"They were never kisses, Jenny. Not like this. Not a whole-body sensation. *These* are kisses. The ones I've been waiting for."

That was either the cheesiest or most romantic thing she'd ever heard. As he kissed her again, she decided it was romantic. Definitely romantic.

* * *

"There's going to be a five-day stretch at Christmas where I'll either be in the Netherlands or on the road," Dylan said, his mind veering from the movie. He'd quickly grown used to seeing Jenny several times a week, and never wanted to leave her. He was starting to see a future beyond hockey—a future where he'd find a new place to belong and build a family with the woman he loved.

"I'm going to miss your cranky face," Jenny said, gripping his chin in her hand. She was leaning against him, their movie interrupted so many times Dylan had lost track of the plot. She turned in his embrace, her lips landing on his. He didn't know how long Gramps' bingo night would last, but every minute alone with Jenny was a blessing.

"Oh, speaking of Christmas, I have something for you." Jenny popped up from the couch, the material of her dress's skirt flipping around her shapely calves. She'd kicked off her cowboy boots ages ago, and she padded down the hall in tall Christmas tree socks that didn't go with her dress one bit.

She returned a moment later with a box wrapped in green foil, with a red silky ribbon tied around it. She suddenly held it to her chest. "Should we wait until Christmas?"

"Actually, I got you something, too," Dylan admitted. He'd studiously not been thinking about the present, fearing he was moving too fast with his gift, that it was too extravagant and filled with expectations. It had only been two and a half weeks since they'd met, but it felt like so much more time had passed. He was ready to take big steps with Jenny, but knew he could easily spook her if he jumped all the way in like he wanted to.

And this gift…it was jumping all the way in.

He sat up, grabbing his jacket from the nearby armchair, doubting himself. He reached into the inside pocket, then presented Jenny with an envelope. "This was a spur-of-the-moment decision this afternoon. I hope…" He considered the plain envelope. "Well, just open it and don't freak out, okay?"

Jenny frowned, then brightened, putting on a silly act. "Oo! An envelope." She turned it over, jamming her thumb under the flap. "Is it something I can wear?" She tucked one leg under her, cozying close again.

"No hints."

"None? Wow, you're strict."

She ripped open the envelope, freeing the folded reservation confirmation.

"What's this?" Her face scrunched in confusion as her eyes skimmed the page. She looked up at him, then back at the paper. "A trip for two? For New Year's?"

"I know. It's too much, too soon," Dylan said, reaching for the trip confirmation.

Jenny leaned back, pulling her hand toward her chest, blocking him from snatching the paper. "It's unexpected, that's all."

He reached for it again. "And too soon."

"Are you changing your mind, Dylan O'Neill?" she asked.

"I want to spend more time with you, and I thought a getaway before I return to the ice would be nice. I can only take two days off, but there would be no distractions. It would be just you and me."

He could see a million thoughts running through her mind as she considered what this trip might mean.

"I can cancel."

She snatched the paper to her chest again, giving him a glare as he ripped a corner. "Don't you dare."

"Jenny." He'd screwed up and she wasn't letting it go or letting him fix it.

"Just…" She pressed a palm against his thigh and inhaled. "Relax. It's good. I appreciate it and think it could be fun." Her expression softened. "But this is a big step in our relationship."

"I know." He couldn't explain the surety he felt. He only hoped she'd soon feel the same way.

Her gaze locked on his and he glimpsed the fear. A trip like this was making a statement, and it was beyond just having fun together.

"It's too soon," he said, his chest tightening.

She started to protest, but he continued, determined to make this something that wouldn't freak her out in any way. "There's a gap in games near the end of February. Lots of players are slipping away for a few days. Why don't we change the dates and go for our birthdays instead?"

The skin around Jenny's eyes softened and her lips curved in relief—or maybe approval for his amended plans, he wasn't sure which. "Yeah? Would that be okay?"

"Yes, of course. I just want to be with you."

She leaned against his arm, hugging it as she smiled, her mouth close to his. "Then I would be delighted to go to Indigo Bay with you and stay in a beautiful beach cottage and cele-brate our birthdays."

"Consider the dates changed." He kissed her slowly, trying to infuse his relief and everything else he was feeling through his kiss. He wanted to make sure she knew exactly where he stood on all things Jenny Oliver related.

The kiss ended and Jenny smiled at him, seeming slightly dazed. Then she brightened with a gasp, pushing away from his chest. "We almost forgot *your* gift."

She shifted, reached to pick up the beautifully wrapped item, then stopped. She turned back uncertainly. "Um. Mine isn't…"

"I went over the top," he assured her.

"I didn't peg you as the fancy gift guy. But I probably should have. And because we've only been together a short time, I wasn't really sure what level of present to get you. Especially with you being rich and famous and able to buy anything you want… So this is…" She exhaled, looking at the box with what appeared to be dread.

"I'm sure I'll love whatever you got me."

She shook her head, biting back a smile. "You won't. You really won't."

He reached past her, snatching the wrapped box. "And I'm not usually a big fancy gift guy. I just heard about the trip today, when Miranda was telling us about the silent auction items for the Dragons' gala. A bunch of guys were arguing over who was going to win it, so I pulled out my phone and booked it for us without even thinking. I'm sorry. Next time I'll ask first."

She smacked his leg. "Don't you dare be like that. The trip is very sweet. And you should know by now that I love spending time with you. Our little getaway will be really special, and without you pulling the pin for us, I would have found a thousand excuses not to go. But I am going to go on this trip in February. And I am going to have fun with my boyfriend."

"Boyfriend, huh? We're official?"

"That gift locked you in, buddy. Good luck getting rid of me now."

"I promise I won't try very hard." He waved the box in his hand. "Do I get to open my substandard present now?"

She groaned, her dramatically sad eyes aimed at the box in his grip. "It really is substandard. I'm so sorry." Her shoulders drooped and she gave him a cute frown, then covered her face with her hands. "Open it."

"What is it?" He pulled at the bow, unraveling the beautiful ribbon, the box heavier than he'd expected.

"No hints." She peeked at him through her fingers as he tore the paper. "You're going to hate it."

He opened the gift and was met with a neatly folded pair of Wrangler jeans, a favorite brand among the local cowboys. Dylan glanced at Jenny. She was biting her bottom lip, shoulders shaking with repressed laughter, her blue-green eyes apologetic and very amused.

He stood up and unfolded the jeans. A small toy truck fell out of the pocket.

"Just a little something to help you fit in," she said innocently.

Unsure how to react, he wordlessly picked up the truck and set it gently on her coffee table.

"Try them on. I had to guess your size."

With a loud grumble, Dylan took the jeans to the bathroom, stripping off his own pants before shaking his head at the fresh denim in his hands. He slid into them, frowning at the unfamiliar snugness against his thighs and other areas. Even though his stomach was flat from the ruthless amount of crunches he had to do as part of training, he still had to pull in a deep breath to do up the fly. Definitely tight. There was no way he was ever going to wear these. Not if he wanted to have children.

He stepped out of the bathroom, giving Jenny an unimpressed glare. He could barely even walk right.

She fell over sideways on the couch, holding her gut as loud guffaws broke free.

"You like what you see?" He lifted his arms and turned slowly, presenting a full 360 degree view. He exaggerated the tightness, stiffly walking bowlegged toward her.

She tumbled off the couch, then stood, coming over to him. "They look so sexy on you. Your thighs are *built*." She ran her hands over the waistband of the jeans, admiring him, the mirth gone. "You're one hot package, Dylan O'Neill."

She had to be kidding. She *liked* him in these? They were awful.

Jenny hooked her fingers through his belt loops and tugged him in closer, snagging a kiss. "These are a gag gift."

He exhaled in relief, wrapping his arms around her.

"I'm sorry I didn't get you something real."

He slid a hand through her hair, giving her a gentle kiss. "If I have you, I don't need anything else."

CHAPTER 9

"Any luck on the dating front, Gramps?" Jenny teased her grandfather as she wiped down the counter and collected their burger wrappers. True to her promise, Mrs. Fisher had sent a salad in Jenny's lunch order. But to Jenny's surprise, Gramps had eaten it without complaint.

"My luck's not as good as yours," he said with a wink. "No rich hockey players chasing me down for a kiss."

Jenny laughed, blushing. It turned out that Gramps hadn't slept peacefully through the recent middle-of-the-night bake-off and had teased her plenty about her shenanigans.

But what he said was true. She was being chased, quite happily, by a professional hockey player. She still couldn't quite wrap her head around that surprising turn of events.

Dylan and Gramps hadn't met yet though. Last week Dylan had fallen asleep on the couch by the time Gramps had come home from bingo, and the couple of dates they'd squeezed in before their busy Christmas week had been quick with Dylan and Gramps passing like ships in the night.

Suddenly, her grandfather seemed to be developing a social life.

"You really need to meet him. He's pretty special."

Jenny wasn't used to being love-bombed, which was quite likely what Dylan was doing. Over-donating to the hampers and the Wylder's animal rescue, and then giving her a trip to Indigo Bay, South Carolina? She could get used to his love bombs. Add in their long string of text messages, the visits, and swoonalicious kisses and she was smitten. He was such a good man, too. So thoughtful and kind. Just that morning, he'd sent an apple pie out to her because he knew her grandfather liked them.

There was no hope for her. She'd allowed herself to fall for the guy—hard—even though she knew there was a very good chance he'd soon be traded.

But it wasn't just Dylan's thoughtfulness or his generous gifts that was warming her heart. It was the way he wanted to spend time with her, the way he fit into her life as if he belonged there. They'd been an item for less than a month and she already couldn't imagine her life without him. He made her feel alive, and she wanted to see the world with him. She wanted him at her side as they shared their adventures. And that made this week apart so much harder to bear.

Dylan had tried to convince her to come to his games and sleep on his couch so they could hang out more. But this year, she and Gramps were hosting the family Christmas, which was in two days. There'd be a dozen of them: her returning parents, her brothers and their families and then herself and Gramps. On top of that, she was holding her annual pre- and post-Christmas sale in the shop and was helping out at several community events. There was no way she could tag along in Dylan's life this week, even though she longed to be with him.

"The woman across the street and I had a nice chat this morning," Gramps was saying. Days ago, he'd finally taken her a fresh batch of welcome cookies after a lot of badgering on Jenny's part.

"Oh?"

"I helped her put up her Christmas decorations."

"Were you on a ladder?" Jenny asked, her heart hammering as she imagined what could have gone wrong, over in the now heavily decorated yard across the street.

He hushed her. "It was fine. She's a few years younger than me. She insisted she do the climbing." Gramps tipped his head thoughtfully to the side. "I'm not sure about her cooking, though."

"You don't like it?"

Gramps made a noncommittal sound.

Jenny wondered if his little chat with Emily had turned into something more. If Gramps found a special someone, she'd feel less worried if she started going to away games with Dylan like he'd hinted she could.

She pulled out the apple pie Dylan had sent to her via Daisy-Mae. "Dylan sent this for you."

"Pie?" Gramps lit up like a kid at Christmas. "Oh, I do like that boy of yours."

She dished them both slices. "So tell me more about Emily's cooking. What don't you like about it?" She ate a bite of apple pie, her eyes closing in bliss. She didn't know where Dylan shopped, but the flaky crust was incredible.

"I haven't tried it yet, but she seems to favor steamed broccoli a lot." He was almost finished his slice of pie already, the dessert disappearing in several quick bites. "You know how I feel about my vegetables. It's like cleaning the bathroom. Leave it as long as you can."

"How do you know all of this about her cooking if you haven't eaten her food?"

"Well, I see it through the ol' binoculars." Gramps sat back proudly.

Jenny sputtered. "You're spying on her?"

"Her kitchen is on the front of her house. It's like an invitation," he replied indignantly. "When the lights are on, I can see right in." He lowered his voice and lifted his white eyebrows. "Be glad it's not her bedroom."

"You're lucky she hasn't noticed you spying on her and called Sheriff Johnson."

"Oh, don't make such a fuss. She doesn't even know."

"That's creepy, Gramps!"

"So I should tell her then?"

"No, you need to stop."

"You're always telling me I should find someone. I was just following your advice. Getting to know her and all."

"Stalking and spying was *not* a tip from me! Go over there and chat with her like a regular human being."

"But you stalked Dylan online. How is this different?"

Jenny felt her face go red. "That's *not* the same thing, Gramps. He puts that info out on social media for people to see." Okay, so he'd only posted about five things, three years ago on his social accounts. As a result, she may also have set up what she privately called a Dylan Spotting alert to notify her when he was mentioned in the news. But that was only because she wanted to understand what was going on in his professional life, as well as with the trade talks. She also might be a tiny bit curious about whether she ever got mentioned. So far, she hadn't been.

But she had noticed an uptick in his mentions in articles, as well as photo postings, since his cast had come off. There'd been one of him in the Dragons' offices, scowling beside Rylnn's dad, Landon the goalie. Then another one a few days later, with him scowling at the camera. But this time, he was all dressed up in a sharp suit, looking hot at an away game.

Gramps crossed his arms. "Looks like stalking to me."

"It's different."

"Hypocrite." Gramps served himself a second serving of pie. "Be sure to send Dutch Boy my thanks."

"I will."

"When do you see him again?"

"After Christmas."

"That long, eh?"

"Yeah. It'll be good though. A chance to recenter."

"You need recentering, do you?"

"No," she sighed, suddenly glum. She missed Dylan. They'd been moving fast, swirling like a tornado into each other's lives, deeper and deeper. She'd thought a few days apart would give her perspective, and it had. But it hadn't brought the insight she'd expected. She'd expected to realize that she needed to get over her infatuation and slow things down because this wasn't anything special. Instead, the time apart was only helping her realize how deeply she believed in the words he'd shared at Thanksgiving: *If you love someone and they're important to you, you find the time. You always find the time."*

She wasn't sure if they were in love, but she did feel as if she was important to him. And maybe she was more than just a way to keep himself entertained while his foot healed. He was planning beyond that with their trip to Indigo Bay.

Was it possible that Dylan O'Neill was really and truly crushing on her, and that she was more than someone he'd picked up to help him pass the time?

* * *

Dylan's crazy Christmas had come and gone and he was finally home from the Netherlands and last night's home game. For the past five days of the so-called 'dark zone', where his and Jenny's schedules didn't mesh, he'd caught himself checking his watch numerous times to see when he could hit the road to go see her. Even when he was in the Netherlands visiting family or in the middle of watching last night's game, she was the only thing on his mind. It was the same all day today, knowing that since it was Sunday, Jenny's store was closed and she probably had free time. But his day, which had originally been a day off, had become locked up tight with meetings, physical therapy, training, a last-minute practice and finally an evening flight up north for tomorrow's away game. It had all gotten so out of hand, he hadn't even taken the time to shave that morning.

Their five days apart were stretching into seven. Seven days.

The jokes and quiet moments of contentment just weren't the same via digital connections.

And so that was why he was in his car, rolling into Sweetheart Creek, the fatigue of the past few days fading as he anticipated seeing his girlfriend. It was also why he'd shut a meeting down early, and why he'd begged Coach Louis for an unorthodox favor, knowing that just asking for it could put him on Coach's hit list.

He probably should have warned Jenny he was coming, but he'd wanted to surprise her.

He parked his Cadillac in front of her country house—or her sugar cookie country house as she liked to call it—noting that this might be the first time he'd actually seen it before the sun set—which would be happening in approximately thirty minutes.

As he shut off his car, he spied movement at the edge of the house, then saw his girlfriend carrying something in the hem of her untucked plaid shirt, carefully pulling bits of straw from her thick hair. He chuckled and hopped out to go help her, a large bag of takeout in hand.

He waited for her moment of recognition and was rewarded with a giant sunny smile and a little leap before she jogged across the lawn to meet him.

"You're sure difficult to get rid of," she whispered, rolling up onto her toes for a kiss.

"Obviously you're not trying very hard." He rested a hand on her lower back, drinking her in.

"Thank goodness I keep failing. And hey, I thought you were busy today?" She lifted her face to his. "And another kiss, please. I missed you." He dropped a slow, easy kiss that felt so right, she loosened the grip on her shirt and almost lost her collection of fresh eggs. She looked down at them. "I should take these inside."

"My meeting ran short," he explained as they cut across the grass to the front door.

"Who'd you have to murder to make *that* happen?"

He smirked, holding the door open for her and gently plucking a bit of straw from her shirt as she passed.

"How long can you stay?" She frowned adorably at him in the home's entry, confusion setting in. "Wait. Don't you have a flight tonight?"

"Since I'm not dressing for the game, Coach Louis said I can fly in tomorrow morning." That had been the favor.

"I thought you said he doesn't let players do that?"

"Usually, he's super strict about that rule."

"Huh." Jenny stared at him for a moment, then jerked as though something had hit her. "Isn't hockey always supposed to come first?"

"Yes." Although he was finding that he didn't want to put it first any longer.

"Yeah. That's what Daisy-Mae told me. You're not going to lose out on something because we couldn't wait two more days to see each other, are you?"

"No," he said, sliding his hands around her waist. "This is all above board."

"Good." Her concern ebbed and she gently cuddled into him, the eggs still nestled in her shirt. "Wanna know a secret?"

"Always."

"I spied your coach mooning over one of my friends at Christmas. Maybe Louis is in love and has gone all soft?"

"I didn't wait around to question him. I just nodded and said 'yes sir' and hightailed it over here."

"You really couldn't wait two more days to see me?" she teased.

"No." His tone was stern, almost grumpy and he worked to soften it, but couldn't. How did she not understand how irresistible he found her?

She laughed softly. "You're such a grumpy guy." She took his chin in her free hand, giving him a tiny shake before lifting her lips for another kiss.

He whispered to her, "Admit it. You secretly enjoy having me around."

"That's no secret."

He pulled her close for a half hug, careful not to crush her eggs, inhaling her hair.

"That you Jenny?" a man called. "I fixed the back door. Just a loose screw in the knob."

"Dylan's here, Gramps!"

The excitement in Jenny's voice warmed Dylan.

"Well, I'll be. The man exists," Garfield Goodwin said, joining them in the entry, his white hair sticking up like he'd been caught in a windstorm. He shook Dylan's hand. "Good to lay eyes on ya. You coming in?"

"Yes, sir. If I'm not interrupting."

"If that's food, you're not interrupting a darn thing."

"Grilled shrimp salad from Oysters." He waved the bag. Jenny had mentioned it was her favorite—their specially seasoned grilled shrimp tossed on a TexMex-inspired salad. Once he'd realized he could squeeze in a Sweetheart Creek trip, he'd had a triple order sent to the rink so he could bring it with him.

The older man, who'd been shuffling toward the kitchen, turned back. "Salad?"

"Yes, sir."

"Well, I guess that'll do. Bring any pie with you, son?"

"No, sir. Not today."

"Well, that's a crying shame. Was a mighty good pie. We'd best order a pizza to go with that salad. Round out the meal a little."

Jenny tried to hide her amusement, silently making a funny face at Dylan.

"That kid at the Watering Hole still delivering?" Gramps asked Jenny.

"I think so." She dutifully set about ordering in a pizza.

"Well, let's dig in before it gets cold," Garfield announced when she was done, sitting down at the kitchen table and giving Dylan an expectant look.

"It started cold, Gramps," Jenny said, getting out dishes so they could split the salad.

"The pizza can be our second course," her grandfather decided.

As they ate, the two filled Dylan in on their holidays and the local gossip. A Christmas tree had fallen over at the kids' Christmas concert, there'd been a runaway bride who'd left the church on horseback, April had thought she was going into premature labor on Christmas Eve but the contractions were just something called Braxton Hicks. Jenny's brothers had decided to arm wrestle at the kitchen table and had broken Jenny's favorite bowl. Mrs. Fisher at the diner had almost set fire to her own hair with the battery-powered Christmas lights she'd put in her teased up, very hair-sprayed do.

As they laughed through the various stories, Dylan sharing a few of his own, he realized how deep Jenny's roots ran in this little town. But hearing Jenny and Garfield tell stories, it felt like Dylan was putting down roots here, too. He was learning more about the people, their personalities and shenanigans, as well as the town, and he could see how it might one day feel a bit like home.

When Garfield finished up an unrelated story about rollercoasters—they'd all agreed they were the best part of amusement parks—Dylan slid a hand over Jenny's. "Will the two of you come watch me play when I return to the ice?"

He'd missed her over the break in the way he'd missed hockey after he'd first broken his foot. He'd felt a little lost, as though something wasn't right in his world and he had a longing for something he couldn't quite place.

And even though he'd just met Garfield, through extension, the man already felt like family. He could think of nothing better than to have the two of them cheering him on as he returned to play in a few weeks.

"Like, in that skybox thing with Miranda and reporters?" Jenny asked, her nose wrinkling.

"The press has their own box." Their team's owner was in the public eye a ton, being a rare female sports team owner, and she was protective of her privacy. There was no way the press would be allowed in her skybox. "Actually, I think some of your friends from town here have watched a game from in there. Cassandra's been in there with Rylnn and her son? And…" He tried to recall who else. "I don't know. Maybe ask around. But it's pretty swank. Free food and merchandise. You name it."

"I couldn't impose like that."

"You wouldn't be. You're my girlfriend." He looked to Garfield who'd been sitting silently. "And a friend. My guests. You can sit anywhere you want. Free tickets. Any time."

Jenny was worrying her bottom lip and he wasn't sure what was holding her back from saying yes. He wanted her there. He wanted to look up and see her cheering him on. He wanted her in his life—his whole life.

Garfield leaned forward. "Will there be pie?"

CHAPTER 10

It was late-January and Dylan was returning to the game he loved. He was dressed and sitting on the bench in case Coach called him out to play, even though it was his first night back. Things were coming together, despite being ten days behind his scheduled return to play, thanks to Karlene being extra cautious with his foot. It had become swollen after the first few times he'd gone hard in practice and she'd pulled back on what he was allowed to do.

But his foot was great. He was great. So what if his foot would be yelling at him by the time the game ended? His girlfriend was in the stands with some friends—Garfield graciously bowing out of tagging along once he learned there'd be no pie—and he was back on the ice. His dream wasn't dead, despite the fears that rookie Leo had started roiling in his head that he was too old to handle any time off the ice and would never recover—a fear that had been amplified with the delayed return to play. But here he was. Dressed in his gear and still holding on to a career he loved. And even better, his Jenny was here to watch him.

In the month since Christmas, they'd settled into a routine of meeting up in Sweetheart Creek or San Antonio for dinner. Or, if time was super tight, they met halfway in some tiny town for a quick bite.

Tonight, though, she was in the stands with some familiar faces from Sweetheart Creek—Athena and her sister Meddy, who Dylan had met once or twice in passing, and Rylnn's nanny Cassandra, who was also their goalie Landon's new girlfriend. The group sat close enough to the ice that he could make out their expressions, as well as catch the way Jenny kept glancing at him.

Her attention drifted his way again, as though magnetized, and he gave her a small nod. Her face lit up, cheeks flushed, then her head ducked shyly.

Jenny shy? Outgoing, vibrant Jenny…acting bashful?

He wondered about that as the game continued. His team appeared to be holding a grudge against the New Jersey forward, with Mullens slamming the player into the boards over and over again. What had he missed while rehabbing his foot?

Dylan glanced at Jenny again and she gave him a cute smile before her eyes darted toward the ceiling at center ice. Then she ducked like she had before.

He lifted his gaze to the giant screen above the middle of the rink. It was broadcasting shots from the crowds here and there and the cameraman had panned to the group of women between plays. A few pink hearts dotted their image before it flickered back to a shot of the ice where Mullens was chasing after the New Jersey player again.

Jenny didn't like being on the screen? He supposed that made sense. Despite her outgoing personality, she did tend to avoid attention. She did a lot for her community in relative secrecy, and maybe the idea of being pointed out as a hockey player's girlfriend was a bit too much for her.

She had to know it didn't have to be crazy, though. Sure, he was in a career where over eighty of his annual work days were televised to millions of people. People could buy jerseys with his name on them, collect and trade cards with his goofy mug on the front and vital statistics on the back. The clusters of reporters outside the rink knew who he was, and that he'd never answer their questions. (They'd tried to hound him about his foot, even going so far as to bust into the secured compound behind the arena where the players parked.) But did they care about his love life?

Probably not.

But Jenny was a good friend of Daisy-Mae's. She'd no doubt heard and seen all the ways life had blown up for her friend since she'd started dating Maverick. Surely Jenny had to understand that Daisy-Mae's relationship was not the standard—the couple had intentionally gone looking for attention as a way to turn the tide on the speculation and rumors following Maverick since his trade from Lafayette. There was no reason for that kind of scrutiny to hit Dylan and Jenny. The two of them would be more like rookie Leo and the team mascot, Violet, another of Jenny's friends from Sweetheart Creek. Quiet. A relationship spent under the radar.

Dating out of the public eye while playing in the NHL was possible, especially if you were someone like him and had a chilly relationship with the press.

But he could also see how one false step could make him lose Jenny, their private relationship quickly belonging to and shaped by the public instead of by themselves. That had happened with a swiftness that still had his head spinning when he'd dated singer Dana Rice while playing for Denver.

Suddenly everything had become about elevating their brands and no longer about them as individuals or as a couple. They were reduced down to their careers and what form of entertainment they could bring to the public.

It had all left a sour impression on him.

There was no way he was going to let that happen with Jenny. He'd keep scowling at the reporters until the cows came home.

"O'Neill!" Coach Louis snapped at him and he jolted from his thoughts, the sounds of the loud arena filling his head. "I said get on the ice!"

* * *

Jenny slipped away from her friends, Athena, Meddy and Cassandra, who were so dazzled by their hockey player crushes they hadn't noticed that she'd fallen behind. Or even that she had her own tried and true crush.

The four of them were somewhere in the arena's basement in a restricted area; the women blowing past security like celebrities visiting an exclusive club. Possibly it was thanks to Athena who worked for the team, or maybe because Cass, who'd come into Jenny's store months ago debating whether to accept a nanny job with Landon, had said yes and now seemed to be in a pretty serious relationship with him.

Her friends had slowed as they approached a cluster of reporters waiting to talk to the players before they made their way to the restricted parking lot behind the arena. Slowly, the three women disappeared into the fray, seeming to already know where to find the men they sought.

Several of her friends still believed what Maverick had told them—that the two had fought all Thanksgiving and didn't like each other. Jenny hadn't bothered to correct them because the few who knew she was dating Dylan asked a lot of questions she couldn't answer. Was she going to leave Sweetheart Creek to be with Dylan? What if he got traded? Didn't he live over an hour away? How would they spend any quality time together?

It hurt her head--and her heart—just thinking about them.

Jenny backtracked, moving away from the group, waiting near a corner just down from the locker room. She leaned against the wall, watching the action. She had twenty minutes before the four of them were meeting up at the car to ride home again.

While she waited for Dylan to come out and meet her, she tried to act like she belonged in the restricted hallway, relieved she wasn't dating Mullens, who had women literally throwing themselves at him. One had flipped up her shirt to have her stomach signed, followed by three more. Earlier, in December, Athena had revealed she was peeved with Mullens. She was working on a second cookbook filled with tips and recipes for athletes and he'd honed in on the project, making it all about him. Essentially, it sounded as though he'd used his celebrity to steal her thunder as well as change the direction of pretty much her entire marketing plan. The man was a show stealer all right, and Jenny bet he overshadowed her bookish friend every time they worked together.

Suddenly the reporters moved forward like a wave, voices raised, cameras and microphones in the air. Jenny fell back again, hugging herself as she stuck by the wall. A few more players came through the crush, though several stayed behind, fielding questions. Maverick answered a few about himself and Daisy-Mae, sliding an arm around her waist, and then a familiar head of unruly sandy hair caught Jenny's attention:

Dylan. He gave a gruff answer to a reporter who flinched, falling back into the mix.

Several more reporters approached Dylan but he continued to move, forcing them to part as he stalked toward her. He was taking up space in a way she'd never seen him do before and very much sending a signal that said *Don't mess with me. Don't talk to me.*

She ducked around the corner, and he caught up with her, grabbing her elbow and hustling her further away from the crowd.

"I'm sorry," she said, hurrying to keep up. "Was I waiting in the wrong place?"

"It's fine." His jaw was tight, his attitude either protective or angry—she couldn't quite tell which. She'd seen him grumpy, quiet, upset, but never this. She wasn't even sure what this *was.*

"Hey, slow down!" He was pulling her so quickly, her cowboy boots were practically sliding out from under her.

He slowed as he tugged them around yet another corner, the din of the reporters shouting questions now muffled as if they were miles away. Dylan, his eyes sharp, glanced through the hallway again. Then he sighed as though exhausted, his body melting against the wall as he propped himself against it. His grip on her elbow released, then his fingers linked through hers. His gaze softened and the tightness at the edge of his mouth vanished like it had never existed.

"Hey," he said softly.

"Hey," she whispered back, her voice breathy, her confusion still swirling.

His eyes roamed over her. Then he was pulling her to him, his arms going around her as he hugged her tight, inhaling her hair before giving her a long, slow kiss.

"I'm glad you came," he murmured.

"Glad you made it worth it by winning."

He let out a huff and tipped his head back. She could have sworn he'd smiled. It was just a flash, but it had been there. A smile for her. Here in the silence of their private hallway in the middle of a NHL arena.

"Feel good to be back out there?" she asked.

"Yeah." His hair was damp from the short time he'd been on the ice, or else from a quick shower and a vigorous toweling. His moments on the ice had been punctuated by how fast and agile he was, zipping around players and proving he belonged on the ice. It had felt like home.

Dylan hooked an arm behind her waist, keeping her against him for another kiss. "You busy later?"

She laughed, gently sliding from his arms.

"Where are you going?" He pulled her back in.

She giggled, letting her body relax against his. It felt like they were sneaking around. But if the rabid reporters, who were frothing just a few corners away, caught them, their relationship would become fodder for the press. She'd seen how Daisy-Mae had lost any sense of privacy. The media even hounded her whenever she tried to work in the city instead of from home.

She'd also noted the way the rink's cameraman who sent footage to the massive TVs that hung above the ice had kept zeroing in on her and her friends. As soon as the world put it together and discovered that she and Dylan were official, it would never be the same. The anonymity and privacy they'd been enjoying up until now would be gone, and she panicked whenever she imagined the untrue and unkind things they might say about her or Dylan and their relationship.

"Hey," Dylan said, pulling her from her thoughts.

She smiled and relaxed. Right now, the future didn't matter. She had safety and privacy and her boyfriend hadn't been traded to a faraway team...yet. They had this moment, and she pulled his lips down to hers, giving him a long, deep kiss filled with promise.

"What are you doing next?" he asked again.

"It's eleven at night," she said with a laugh. "Some people have normal lives, jobs and hours. Plus, I have a big drive home and I work in the morning."

"You're the boss. Blow it off. Crash at my place."

It was tempting. So very tempting.

She raised an eyebrow. "Would you blow off your job?"

He hesitated. "When can you sneak away next? How about Tuesday?"

"This Tuesday?" Still snug in his arms, she played with the thin chain around his neck, which had been a second Christmas gift from her—a real one. "I do have a store that's open weekdays, you know..."

"Just the afternoon," he replied, his voice low and rumbly in the most delicious way. "I have nothing after our morning practice. I want to take you to a few places in the city."

"I've already seen a couple of your favorite restaurants," she teased, curious to hear what he had in mind.

"Outside of restaurants. We'll make an afternoon and evening of it. Would April cover you if you came in after lunch?"

Jenny found herself nodding. "Yeah, I'll ask."

"Good." He nuzzled her cheek with his nose. "I want you to get to know me in my world."

She laughed and gestured around the corner to where the press was still mobbing players. "Hon, I'm sorry, but your world is nuts."

The edge of his mouth quirked up, but his eyes remained serious. "I meant my everyday world. The boring, dry, colorless world I suffer in whenever I'm not with you."

She huffed a laugh at his exaggeration. She didn't know what he had in mind for their next date, but she doubted it was as mundane as their last date, which had been a trip to the grocery store because she'd run out of milk. "You really know how to sell a girl on something."

"If you see my sad little lonely world, you'll feel compelled to save me, to hang out with me every day."

"You charmer. Where will we go?"

"I'll show you my life."

Well aware that the man had barely even explored his home city thanks to his dedication to hockey and his team, she said softly, "You don't have a life."

"Outside of you and hockey, I don't."

She watched him, her heart increasing its tempo at his seriousness. She slid her arms around his neck, knowing that there was nowhere else she'd rather be than in his life as deeply as he was in hers. "Show me everything that's you, Dylan."

CHAPTER 11

Jenny slipped her hand through Dylan's as they walked through the Alamo, an old Spanish mission in the heart of what was now downtown San Antonio. Cannons and guns, sun-bleached stone buildings, history, and late January's unpredictable Texas temperatures kept them company as they wandered.

Jenny tugged the sleeve of her sweatshirt over her free hand as they slowly wound their way through a shaded area, in and out of buildings and around the grounds until they stopped in front of Jenny's favorite sculpture: Davy Crockett.

"I've heard of this guy," Dylan said, reading the inscription. "I didn't know he was part of the Texas Revolution."

"Most people think of him as a frontiersman. Or at least, I used to as a kid until we took a school trip here." Jenny pointed to a grassy area within the compound as they continued their wandering. "Ryan Wylder pulled my ponytail right there and I developed a huge crush on him."

"You still have it?" Dylan asked, his voice slightly wary.

"Nope. He squelched it in junior high."

They walked a little further, the odd person giving Dylan a second glance now and then, as if they were trying to place him. Each time Dylan tensed and changed their direction. Jenny was grateful that hockey was still far behind football in terms of popularity in Texas, meaning he'd only been outwardly recognized once. And that person had simply nodded and said "Good to see you back on the ice."

There'd been no swarming of fans or paparazzi like she'd secretly feared. And even though she'd been on the arena's Jumbotron earlier in the week, today had been just like all of their other dates—quiet and theirs.

"I have a question," she said, her mind trying to put together pieces of Dylan's past and failing.

"What's that?"

"What happened with Dana Rice?"

"With Dana?" His brows shot up and he glanced over at Jenny.

"Yeah. Because I saw a picture from a few years back where you're smiling at the camera." Dana had long blond, wavy hair and giant blue eyes, and a slender frame. She was a gorgeous, talented singer who appeared more than happy to be in the spotlight. "You didn't look as though you minded being photographed then." Unlike in any of the more recent photos she'd seen whenever her phone had pinged with another Dylan Spotting automatic notification.

He blinked a few times, his frown deepening. "Well, the press got involved in our relationship, and it started to feel like everything we did was for the public. Everything became orchestrated."

"Oh."

"We were both using each other, I think. I don't know. A lot of things happened."

For a while, Jenny had feared Dylan would be traded back to his old team and that Dana would sweep him up again. It sounded like Jenny could cross that irrational worry off her list and just fret over the idea of him being traded instead.

"It was a good lesson, though," Dylan said thoughtfully.

"In what way?"

"That I shouldn't let others inflate my ego or to start expecting things I hadn't earned."

"Like what?" She couldn't imagine Dylan acting entitled.

He waved off the question. "It doesn't matter. But essentially, I don't think I should be treated any differently than anybody else, just because I'm privileged enough to play for the National Hockey League." His shoulders had become stiff, his tone almost curt.

She could tell his sense of fairness had been rattled somewhere along the line, and she wondered what exactly had gone down.

They walked in silence, passing a family of four in an old, narrow corridor, its arches open to the mission's courtyard to their left.

They exited the Alamo, lowering their sunglasses as they moved back into the bright, unsheltered afternoon sun.

"Daisy-Mae was saying how important publicity is for players so they're offered marketing deals outside of hockey. You don't worry about that? Or do you already have deals in place?"

Daisy-Mae was in the city today, working at the rink, and Jenny hoped for her friend's sake it was all going well. The recent reporter feeding frenzy around her and Maverick still hadn't died off. Then again, Daisy-Mae, a former beauty queen, knew how to strut her stuff and handle reporters.

Jenny would probably turn red and babble nonsensical things if their roles were reversed.

"I'm happy with what I have," Dylan said. "I can retire tomorrow if need be."

"Can you really? Wow." Jenny leaned into him, curious how he envisioned his retirement. "Who are you outside of hockey? Would you miss it? Be bored?"

He looked at her, hooking his arm through hers as they meandered. "I'd be the same guy. Just less busy. And I don't think I'd be bored because I'd like to have a family." The way he was watching her intently made her feel as though he was asking her something, even though he wasn't.

"It would be a big change," he said. "The team is my family. My community. I'd miss it all. But since my injury, I've been learning that maybe those things exist outside of hockey, too. Maybe I wouldn't combust in a cloud of identity loss."

She smiled softly, knowing he wouldn't. He fit into her life and world like he belonged there. He was genuine and kind. The type of man who would fit in anywhere if he just gave himself a chance.

"I'd combust in a cloud of identity loss without my store," she admitted. "Or the town. Who am I outside all of that stuff?" She sighed, the answer always elusive.

But it wasn't just a matter of who she'd be if she left Sweetheart Creek. It was also a question of what she'd do and who'd look in on Gramps. And then there were all the other little things... Like, what would happen to her store and the families who depended on her to clear their diner tabs. Or what about the teens who'd get nothing but body wash, socks and perfume in their Christmas hampers? It was her community and her extended family. She couldn't simply abandon them so she could go on an adventure she wasn't even certain she truly wanted.

"Who says we have to be someone?" he asked, taking her hand. "Maybe we just need to exist and be happy and have lots of babies."

She laughed. "Perpetuate the species and all that?"

"I'm planning to have enough kids to field our own hockey team."

She felt a wash of heat at his use of 'our' when referring to his offspring. Did he really want five or six kids?

"What would you do if you retired?" she asked, trying to concentrate on their conversation rather than whether or not he actually wanted *that* many children. "Work? Play golf all day? Change diapers?"

"Definitely stay home with the kids."

"No. You're kidding. Really?" Her heart felt like it had taken a fatal shot as she imagined him with his own kids, letting them dress him up as Rylnn had at Maverick's place, back in November. She could see Dylan driving their future children to hockey practice, coaching and teaching them how to lace up their own skates. The works. Even rocking a baby while he burped it in the kitchen in the wee hours of the morning. It all came to her in a heart-squeezing flash.

"Really," he said. "That's after I spend a year or two traveling and eating whatever I wanted without worrying that Athena will yell at me. Basically, I'd do all those things I've been putting off or have been too busy to do. Then after that, I'd probably put my business degree to good use and harass my investment and property managers with all of my annoying, irrelevant book knowledge." He winked at Jenny. Over time, he was revealing more and more of his dry sense of humor and she loved it. Would he ever reveal a trait she didn't adore?

He guided them onto a patch of grass by the sidewalk, lining them up so the Alamo's entrance was at their back. "Want a selfie?"

"Of course I do. But don't scowl!" She cozied into his side, smiling, relaxed and content with the day and getting to know Dylan better. He reached out a long arm, snapping a photo.

"Did you smile?" She snatched for his phone, eager to see what he'd captured. She pretended to pout as she looked at the picture. "You never smile."

"I am smiling."

She studied the photo. His demeanor was relaxed, and he wasn't frowning. For Dylan, yes, he was smiling. She tapped on the image, sharing it to herself via text message, then handed him back his phone.

"So you're happy not being in the spotlight?" she confirmed as they headed to his car.

"Yes." His certainty left no doubt, and she let out a breath of relief.

After seeing what Daisy-Mae was going through, she'd been starting to think she'd need to learn how to handle fame, which was a daunting and terrifying prospect.

"So, Dylan O'Neill," she asked, her voice like an announcer's, "are you telling us you still play hockey for the love of the game and not for the multi-million-dollar paychecks and the opportunity to have women throw themselves at you?"

Over the roof of his car, he simply shook his head, giving her a dry look.

"Do I look like Mullens?" he muttered, referring to the team's most gregarious player.

Honestly, Jenny could tell Dylan loved the game, and a

warm feeling expanded through her chest whenever she thought about how he'd looked while playing. He was at home on the ice. He was relaxed, yet intense. And he made it look so darn easy. Nothing should ever take that away from him. And while his healed foot was a double-edged sword—meaning the trade talks had amplified—it also showed that he hadn't lost a career that obviously meant so much to him.

"So you really have retirement set up already?" she asked, feeling curious. When her accountant and bookkeeper got after her about formulas and profit margins, her mind started to act like a caffeinated toddler who'd missed nap time. She had her systems for her business, and automatic withdrawals for her retirement fund, but she honestly wasn't a hundred percent sure when she could actually retire. Running a somewhat young business, there were just too many variables for her to be able to pinpoint a date.

The lines around Dylan's mouth deepened, the softness gone. "In hockey, you have to be prepared to have it all yanked out from under you at any time."

Seeing the way his shoulders tensed, she understood the toll his injury had taken on him in terms of his concerns for his career and future. It was incredibly unfair that something like an accidental bone break or the natural process of aging could take him away from a career he'd spent more years working toward than actually enjoying.

She sat in the passenger seat, turning to face Dylan as he started the car. "What's next on our date's agenda?"

"It's a secret."

"A matinee movie?"

"Why? Are you short on time?"

"For you, Dylan O'Neill? I have all day."

He shot her a hot gaze that pooled heat in her stomach and

she smiled as they pulled out into the slow Tuesday afternoon traffic, off to their next adventure.

* * *

Dylan drove up to the manned gate that led to the private parking lot at the back of the Dragons' arena. Jenny sat up straight in her seat. "Why are we here?"

He nodded to the attendant who let them through the gates.

"Have you ever played hockey before?" Dylan asked Jenny.

She laughed nervously. "I don't know how to skate. We're going on the ice? With other players?" She covered her face, her voice rising. "Oh no. Are you going to shoot slapshots at me to see if I'd be a good goalie for your future family team? Because I wouldn't. I bruise easily and am afraid of flying pucks. And footballs. And baseballs."

He chuckled, delighted she'd been envisioning a future together where they were building their own hockey team. "Why would you be goalie?" The kids would be on the ice. He'd be coaching and she'd be cheering them all on and doing what she pleased.

"A team needs a goalie," she explained, "so that means six kids to make a team." She had uncovered her face. "That's a *lot*. I'm confident I'd top out at four."

He hid his smile. "Duly noted." He parked the car near the doors, surprised to see so many vehicles in the lot, seeing as the players had the day off. There must be another press conference going on. "And as for skating, I'll teach you." They couldn't have her not knowing how to skate if they were thinking of building a team.

He reached across the console, giving her knee a squeeze. "It'll be just us on the ice. Trust me, it'll be fun."

He parked the car, grabbed her hand and let them into the building with his pass. They wove their way through various hallways, past a full meeting room, and through several locked doors until they were deep in the arena. He unlocked the equipment room, heading to the shelves of skates. When he'd been in the minors, there had been no surplus and he still had moments of wonder at how well-equipped this team was. In front of him was a shelf with thousands of dollars' worth of equipment just sitting, waiting to be needed.

"What size are your feet?"

"Eight."

"Let's try a seven in men's." He took a pair from the labeled shelf and handed them to Jenny. "Sorry, we don't have any ladies' skates. Although maybe hockey skates are unisex. I don't actually know. My sister never wanted to skate."

Dylan helped her lace up and then onto her feet.

She wobbled a little, then took a few small steps. "Not too bad."

"A natural. My skates are in the locker room."

He led them down the hall, Jenny hesitating outside the door with the sign that said Private: Dragons Only. "What if someone's getting dressed?"

Dylan opened the door and hollered inside, "Everyone decent?" Hearing no reply, he pushed the door wider, allowing Jenny into the team's inner sanctum. "If anyone asks, you've never been in here."

"Deal. And if anything slips, I'll say that Athena or Daisy-Mae told me. Or Violet," Jenny said, taking in the room, the open lockers with waiting jerseys labeled with famous names.

"Seriously. Do the Dragons only date my friends or something?"

"We seem to have a thing for the women of Sweetheart Creek." He pulled her close, giving her a quick kiss before grabbing his skates and lacing up.

He winced as he tightened the laces over the arch of his right foot. It still wasn't particularly happy when he squeezed into his skates, and time didn't seem to be helping. Karlene told him to be patient. It was probably bone spurs and scar tissue.

The end of his career.

He stood, re-joining Jenny. It felt weird to be in skates and jeans. He felt a bit like a tourist or a noob.

Although, getting all geared up would have been even more ridiculous.

He grabbed two hockey sticks, shoved a puck in his back pocket, and led them down the hall to the rink's gate. He leaned the sticks against the inner glass, then lifted the heavy metal handle with a clank, releasing the half door. A few security lights lit up the ice and he was tempted to turn on all the big lights as well as some music. Then again, it was smarter to lie low. As a member of the team, he could come skate whenever there was free ice time, but he wasn't sure what the rules were about allowing his girlfriend to tag along on a pair of skates belonging to the Dragons.

He stepped onto the ice, then turned and held his hands out for Jenny. She bit her bottom lip and clutched him, tentatively placing her right foot on the ice. So far, so good.

Then she was on the ice, her momentum pushing him to glide backward, pulling her along while she laughed. She leaned forward and back wildly as she tried to find her balance.

"I've got you." He skated backward, her hands in his, the familiar sound of metal blades carving the ice filling the air. He could see why they always went skating in the movies. It was cheesy, but romantic and a very good excuse to wrap his arms around his girlfriend whenever she wobbled.

He locked his gaze on hers as he continued to guide her. "Tell me a secret."

Her eyes sparkled and she laughed. "I used to dye my hair blond." She let go of one of his hands to try and gesture to her hair, but wobbled, clinging to him again. "This is my natural color."

"Yeah? Why'd you try being blond?"

"Everyone says they have more fun, but obviously that's wrong. Look at me now!"

He huffed a soft chuckle, the cool arena air making Jenny's cheeks rosy. She'd never been more beautiful to him than she was at this moment, and he'd always thought she was plenty beautiful.

"Okay, tell me one," she said.

"A secret?"

"Yeah."

"When I got my first NHL paycheck, I thought they'd made a mistake and paid me for the whole year instead of just the month. Even though I knew what I was supposed to earn, I'd never seen that kind of money before."

She was watching him, her skating and balance becoming more natural and smooth. "What a feeling that must have been."

"I still haven't totally gotten used to it," he admitted.

Once Jenny was able to stand on her own, he offered her a stick. She clung to it, pressing it down onto the rink's surface for support, tentatively skating down the rink like a fawn learning how to use its legs.

"Try and catch up, O'Neill!" She cackled as she went past, starting to get the hang of making gliding strokes with her skates. She whooped as her feet slipped too far apart, recovering with help from her stick.

He breezed past her, backward.

"Show off!" She wobbled precariously as she brought her skates back together, stopping her forward momentum by slamming her stick against the ice. "You make this look so easy."

They skated a few more laps, took a few shots on goal, Jenny cheering wildly when she finally got one in, the concentration and glee on her face adorable. She was a fast learner and he could see with a lesson or two she'd soon be zipping around as if she'd been born to it.

He skated over, catching her in a giant hug. She squealed as her skates left the ice, him holding them up as they glided across the frozen surface.

He nuzzled her ear, whispering the three secret words he'd feared he'd never find someone to say them to.

* * *

As Dylan released Jenny's feet from the skates, her mind whirled and buzzed. Dylan loved her. Dylan O'Neill, NHL player, sexy, studly, grumpy man, her boyfriend, the man of her dreams, actually loved her.

He'd whispered the words as he swept her toward the boards, bringing them off the ice. She'd been so stunned, wobbling on her feet when he'd put her back down on firm ground that she hadn't even mustered a moment to say it back.

"All set," he said, pinching the skate's blades between his fingers and running them down the length, clearing off the bits of ice shavings that clung to the metal. He set the skates down in a pair and looked up at her from his crouched position.

He hadn't waited, hadn't expected her to say 'I love you' back to him. He'd just said it and then had moved on.

She leaned forward on the bench, clasping his face and giving him a big kiss.

She held him close after the kiss ended, summoning her courage, knowing that as soon as she repeated those three words back to him, they'd have moved beyond something fun and into a real relationship, one that might have long-term potential.

"I love you, too."

And then he smiled. An actual, genuine smile that turned the corners of his mouth up in the most dazzling, wonderful sight she'd ever seen in her entire life. It was even better than the Denver one she'd seen online. Way better.

"Let's go get something to eat," he said, standing and pulling her to her feet. "I made us a reservation."

"Fancy." She took his hand as he led them back out of the arena, reversing their earlier maze-like moves, and walking back through Employee Only doors. "Thank you for showing me your world. It was fun."

"I loved it." He paused and planted a gentle kiss against her temple.

This day, this man, was heaven. Pure heaven.

He opened the doors to the parking lot and the loud

sounds of a crowd assaulted her ears. Jenny leaned closer to Dylan who paused over the threshold, assessing the situation. His car was only a few dozen feet away, but it was in the midst of the crowd which was surrounding someone.

"What's going on?" she asked, trying to peer around his shoulder.

He shook his head. "I don't know."

"Is that Daisy-Mae?" Jenny rolled up onto her tiptoes, squinting at the large cluster of reporters and photographers. They were crushed in a circle with what appeared to be her friend in the center.

"And Miranda?" Dylan added for her benefit, "The team's owner."

"I know. She bought the Johnson's old place outside of town."

She glanced at Dylan, taking cues from him. Did they venture out into the masses or retreat back inside? She'd never seen reporters act quite like this before and she wasn't sure if their pushing and shoving and shouting was normal or even safe.

Above the din, the voice of one lone security guard repeated that this was a secure area and those without passes should leave immediately. Jenny caught a few of the reporters' questions as they edged their way toward the car.

"When are you due, Daisy-Mae? Is the baby Maverick Blades's?"

"Miranda! Is dating Dakarai Morisette a conflict of interest? Will you step down from your management role with the team's charity?"

"Miranda, are you pregnant?"

"Daisy-Mae, what do you have to say about Maverick and Reanna?"

"It's a bloodbath," Jenny said with shock, feeling for the two women who were trapped at the center of it. It was like a school of piranhas had been thrown a piece of meat.

"How did they even get back here?" Dylan asked, pulling her toward his car. "It's supposed to be secure."

"Where's the rest of security?" Jenny asked, her anger growing. This was like her own worst nightmare coming true for two women she considered friends. She'd known things were getting wild with Daisy-Mae and Maverick in the news, but she hadn't realized that the escalation looked quite like *this*.

Dylan let go of her hand, directing her to move past some reporters and between two cars. She stopped between the bumpers and turned to Dylan. "We have to help them."

Now that they were in the fringe of the crowd, she could see the women trying to edge their way toward the safety of the building, their one security guard doing an ineffective job of clearing a path. There were just too many pushy, desperate people to fight.

Dylan slipped Jenny his car keys. "Wait for me in the car."

She nodded as a scuffle broke out beside them, two reporters shouldering each other to the point that it looked like two football players trying to hold their defensive positions. Then one pivoted his shoulder, giving the other a giant shove as well as sharing some rather choice words. The man crashed into Jenny, and Dylan gripped her hand, attempting to prevent her from falling. His grip failed and she landed awkwardly on her free arm between the cars, striking the hard pavement with a bone jarring hit.

Dylan had her back on her feet before she had a chance to understand what had happened. Then he was in the face of the reporter who'd tumbled against her, his accent thick as he told him exactly how he felt about his actions.

Jenny grabbed Dylan's hand and hauled him the last few feet to Daisy-Mae and Miranda, using her low center of gravity and anonymity to shoulder people out of their path. Dylan, neck red with anger, corralled the three women, barking at the crowd as he worked like a bodyguard to edge them back toward the arena's door. They were jostled and questions were shouted. Someone even called Jenny's name.

Dylan continued to act like a human shield, glowering. Anyone who came close enough to push a microphone or camera in their face was deflected by the hockey player.

Outside the rink doors, Miranda tripped, landing against the wall, hitting the door's security lock with her ready ID card. The light turned green and the latch released. Dylan swung the heavy metal door open and the four of them stumbled into the arena.

Dylan gave a ferocious yank on the door, and any fingers that gripped its edge disappeared before he banged it shut with an echoing finality.

The four of them exhaled loudly, Jenny panting from adrenaline.

"Verdomde gek," Dylan said, translating for the confused women, "Bonkers." Jenny had a feeling there'd been a swear that had gone with the word.

Daisy-Mae was shaking, and Miranda ran a hand up and down the woman's back.

"Is everyone okay?" Dylan asked, his voice too loud for the sudden quiet. His eyes were alert, his shoulders pushed out, ready to take up more space at a moment's notice.

Daisy-Mae and Miranda nodded.

"What was that?" Jenny asked.

Daisy-Mae's smile was tight. "Life after Reanna."

Jenny felt her gut clench, and she whispered, "Are you serious?"

She'd seen the interview last week where the Lafayette owner's wife had ambushed one of Maverick's TV interviews. Reanna had gone on to clear up the rumors between herself and Maverick, but then had dropped a few bombs. It had been a bit of a mess ever since, with the public trying to sort out what was what. And apparently, that involved continuing to badger Daisy-Mae.

"How did they get back here?" Dylan asked. "Were they invited?"

Miranda's voice trembled with rage. "It was a press conference to clear up growing rumors around Maverick being traded back to Lafayette—"

"Which is not going to happen," Daisy-Mae added.

"—and they were not given access to the private lot. I certainly have some very strong words for the security team." Miranda faced Dylan. "Thank you for your help, Dylan."

"Any time."

Miranda turned to Daisy-Mae, fixing her dark topknot with trembling fingers. "Let's go to my office until security can clear the lot."

The two women headed deeper into the arena, their voices rising and falling. Dylan ran a hand down his face, stroking his chin.

Jenny was still shaking from adrenaline.

One of the reporters had known her name. Did that mean things were going to get insane for her, the way they were for Daisy-Mae?

"What do we do now?" Jenny asked, staring at the gray metal door, knowing there was no way she was ever walking through it again until every last reporter had left. She could still hear voices and the odd clang, as if people were bumping against the door. She shivered.

"Are you okay?" Dylan asked, turning back to her. He focused on her, his face pinched with concern as he noticed the rip in her sweatshirt sleeve. "You landed hard."

She paused to consider and realized her left arm didn't feel right. Her fingers tingled and her arm felt strange, sort of like it was confused between aching and feeling fine. "I think I bumped a nerve or something." She shook her shoulder, trying to work out the tingles, but it just made her entire arm feel worse.

"It could be broken." He took her arm, gently probing it.

"It's not." She pulled back. She could move everything— her fingers, wrist, elbow. It just tingled and had a weird achy feeling.

"No, let me see." He held her arm again, rolling up her sweatshirt sleeve to check for swelling and bruising. He was so doting and worried, she felt a flutter of appreciation at having someone looking out for her, protecting her.

Mostly, though, she was embarrassed. She'd crashed to the ground with surprising finality. No bounce. Just an embarrassing, graceless landing between two cars, as if she was a sack of potatoes that had been tossed aside.

"It'll be okay. See?" She waved her arm, wincing as a spear of sharp tingles zinged across her nerves.

"Come on." He turned, moving further into the building again, all solid determination, no crinkling around his eyes or telltale hints of his earlier smile.

"We'll miss dinner." She slowed her pace, but he pulled her along by her good arm, muttering something gruff, his mouth flattening in a very stern way. She was starting to feel the fatigue of the post-excitement rush, and she struggled to keep up with his fast clip. He released her and she slowed.

He was like he was on the ice: a whizz, dazzling her with impossible seeming moves as if gravity and physics weren't real. Were the dates he planned always going to involve him waiting for her to figure it out? Did they have enough common ground outside of sitting on her couch and arguing about cookie sprinkles to make a relationship work?

They approached a flight of stairs and she winced on the first step; her left knee letting her know it had suffered in the fall as well.

Dylan turned back, already near the top. He frowned at her limp and jogged back down, arms out as though he planned to carry her.

"No!" She held out a hand. No way. She sucked in a slow breath. "I can manage. Thank you."

She already felt uncoordinated enough. And embarrassed that she couldn't keep up with her athletic boyfriend. Him carrying her, even though she was legitimately wounded, would be humiliating. Plus, if her strapping hot boyfriend strained at all while carrying her up the stairs, she would simply die.

Her hand started shaking on the railing as she thought about how Miranda and Daisy-Mae had been penned in by the reporters, and the fear she'd felt rip through her when she'd been knocked down. She didn't want to experience any of that ever again, but she knew that by continuing to date Dylan, it was a very distinct possibility.

* * *

"This is Karlene Spragg," Dylan said, ushering Jenny into the Dragons' physical therapist's room. Massage beds, curtained areas, machines on carts, exercise balls, stacks of towels, treadmills and weights filled the large area. It had been his own personal hell over the past several months. "Our team's PT specialist. She said she can take a peek since the team doctor's not here today."

They'd gone deeper into the arena than before, the craziness from outside firmly locked away. There was a quiet hum of activity in the area they were in now, everyone from suits to players going about their business, even though it was close to supper time.

Jenny looked pale and shaky, and he wasn't sure if it was from the fall in the parking lot or the startling exposure to what his life could be like if he stepped back into the limelight with a welcoming smile.

Seeing her fear and how the reporters had disrespected Miranda and Daisy-Mae, there was no way he'd ever go back. He'd keep scowling at every reporter and keep his girlfriend as safe as possible.

Dylan introduced Jenny to Karlene, and as they shook hands, Jenny's head tipped to the side. "Did you go to Sweetheart Creek High?"

Karlene, usually all business, lit up with a smile. "I did! Transferred over from Riverbend for my sophomore year."

Jenny nodded. "Wigmore High fire?" She leaned toward Dylan, filling him in. "Their high school burned down so they all came over to our school. It was all very exciting. So many new boys."

"It's where I met my...Thomas." Karlene's voice trailed off and Dylan's eyes slid to the woman's left hand. It was ringless. She should be wearing two by now since she'd been planning a Christmas wedding last he'd heard. How had he not noticed or asked about her wedding during their many, many appointments over the past several weeks?

He glanced up to catch Karlene's expression, but she continued quickly, her face pleasantly set in that professional way of hers. "So, what brings you in? Dylan said you fell?"

"Got shoved by a reporter," he growled.

"Goodness." Karlene, one hand under Jenny's good elbow, helped her onto her exam table. "Well, let's take a peek and see what's what."

"Really, I think it's fine. Just feels weird." Jenny wiggled her fingers on her left hand to demonstrate and winced. "I appreciate you taking a look, though," Jenny said. Her eyes were big, more blue than green, and she looked small and frightened.

The idea that she'd been hurt by reporters made Dylan so livid, he wanted to rip the curtains down from their rails and destroy every piece of exercise equipment in the room.

"I'm not a doctor," Karlene said smoothly, "but I'll be able to tell if you should seek medical treatment. Let me know if anything hurts." She gently worked her way over Jenny's arm with fingers that seemed a lot more tender than when she was checking over one of the guys on the team.

"Hey!" Jenny said, her voice high with dawning. "You bought a wedding dress from my store, didn't you?"

"I did," Karlene said, her tone distracted.

"It was very beautiful, but I can't recall when your date was?" Jenny asked, her words polite and practiced, the way he heard her speak with customers when he stopped by at the end of her day to pick her up.

"Can you bend your elbow? Any pain?"

Jenny glanced at Dylan and he gave a subtle shrug and

shake of his head. Her guesses were as good as his own when it came to Karlene's missing rings and topic dodging.

"It feels weird," Jenny said, focusing on her hand. "Tingles like an electric eel keeps zipping up and down my arm."

"Paresthesia," Karlene stated, stepping back.

"Is that bad?"

Dylan gripped Jenny's good hand as she paled, inhaling her hair and the scent of cinnamon, trying to contain his anger. He was going to sue the heads off of those two fighting reporters.

Karlene smiled reassuringly. "It's a fancy word for tingles. Looks like it's just bumped and bruised."

"That's all? You're sure?" Dylan asked, his relief so deep it felt unreal. "No chipped bone or anything? Should it be x-rayed?"

"It's presenting like a tweaked nerve that's speaking out and letting her know it's not happy. The tingling should resolve within the next hour or two. If not, or if it bruises horribly or swells up, then go to the emergency room. Otherwise, just a bit of heat for any muscle aches and pains and some ice for the spot where you landed on your arm and you should soon be right as rain."

They thanked Karlene, and in the hallway as soon as the door closed, Jenny turned to him, eyes wide. "I think she was the runaway bride. The one I mentioned after Christmas. You know? That time you brought over shrimp salad."

"What? Karlene?" He frowned, trying to recall Jenny's story from that night.

"Yes! She took the horse from the carriage outside the church and rode off."

Dylan halted, staring at the closed door. "Wait. Karlene did that?"

"Shh!" Jenny hurried them along. "I think so. She said 'her Thomas,' and Thomas McNaughton, whose family owns and runs this massively huge ranch outside town, was supposed to get married last month. So was she. Sweetheart Creek isn't that big. It *has* to be her."

"What a blindside that must have been," Dylan said, shaking his head in wonder, unable to imagine the scope of it all. He slid his arms around Jenny, feeling relief that he had her, that his love was returned, and most of all that she was safe and would be okay.

Jenny, worrying her bottom lip, was looking toward the closed door behind them. "I feel so bad for her. What a Christmas that must have been."

Dylan hugged Jenny closer, careful not to bump her left arm. "I love how much you care about the people in your community. You're a sweetheart."

Her eyes turned upward, a pretty green filled with happiness. Contentment and love. He was such a lucky man. How could that Thomas guy not have noticed such a look missing in Karlene's eyes?

Maybe it had never been there, and Thomas hadn't known to look for it.

Dylan shivered, thinking how he could have ended up in the same shoes if Jenny hadn't come along and shown him what real love felt like. He kissed her, vowing to keep her safe and to protect their love no matter what it took.

Jenny's stomach growled and Dylan checked his watch. "We need to feed you."

Her cheeks turned pink and she shook her head. "I'm okay. And anyway, I doubt it's safe to go out there..."

The worry and fear had returned to her eyes.

He stroked her cheek. "I'm sure Miranda's had the lot cleared and re-secured by now."

"Really, I'm okay."

"You're a bad liar. You're hungry."

"We must have missed our reservation."

"It's okay." He released her and got out his phone, quickly shooting off a text. He shot her a wink. "I know a place."

CHAPTER 12

"*A* hot tub?" Jenny stared at the steam coming out of the small pool built into the expansive back patio at Dylan's townhouse. The whole backyard was a private oasis with lots of sitting areas, a double hammock between two short palms, plenty of landscaping as well as the fully decked out tub that was screened off from the rest of the yard to provide additional privacy.

"It's great for sore muscles. Give me your aches and pains and I'll turn you into a renewed woman."

"That's a mighty promise." A good soak in the heat did look inviting. "But I don't have a bathing suit."

Dylan guided her back into the house and she glanced over her shoulder at the hot tub. It had been sunk into a cedar deck, lanterns crisscrossing the music-filled air above it, and fronded plants surrounded the steaming water to make it feel even more secluded. As they walked up the stone path with inlaid lights along its edges, they passed a lovely reclined sitting area, wide enough to be a bed, peppered with blankets and cushions as it faced an outdoor bar with a television.

"Why do we hang out at my house?" she asked.

"Because it's where you are," he said simply.

"Well, I should have made a point of seeing your place ages ago. It's amazing." When he'd said it was a pit-stop and not a home, she'd half-expected something more dorm-like. Not this little haven.

She paused, glancing back at the blankets, cushions, uncovered hot tub and lit-up lights. "You just leave it all set up like this? What if it rains?"

"I have a household manager. He got his days mixed up and set it all up for me."

"I'm sorry. What did you say? You have a household manager?"

Dylan shrugged and continued moving toward the house.

She jogged across the lush lawn, instantly regretting it as her knee protested the motion. "Like a valet for an 1800s lord?" she asked, catching up.

"A valet?"

"I enjoy reading historicals."

Dylan made a sound that almost sounded like a chuckle. "Well, Jeeves sets this up on my workout days. He knows I'll want to kick back when I get home on the days I'm not heading to Sweetheart Creek."

"*Jeeves?*"

"His real name's Paul."

"How did I not know about all of this?"

Dylan shrugged, looking around as though not seeing it all. "None of this makes it a home."

"I suppose." She took one last wistful look at the yard before joining Dylan through the large glass door that separated the expansive living room from the outdoors. "Do you have a chef as well?"

"Paul cooks for me. He baked that pie I sent for your grandfather."

"Does he clean?"

"No. But he takes care of bills and household maintenance stuff. Laundry, appointments."

Now it made sense how he appeared to have more free time than she did, even though he had an insane hockey schedule. He never seemed to stop by the store to pick something up, or any of those mundane things. She'd just assumed he was more organized than she was.

"This is amazing. It's like having a wife. I want one. Can he rustle me up a bathing suit?"

"Probably."

Jenny peered across the sitting area, trying to see further into the kitchen than the wall of cupboards allowed. "Is he still here?"

"He's starting supper." As though upon cue, a middle-aged man in an apron appeared out of a walk-in pantry in Jenny's line of sight. He saw them and gave a cheery wave. "Chicken enchilada casserole fit the bill?"

"Sounds amazing," Jenny admitted.

"Not allergic to squash or any spices?" he asked.

"Squash?"

"It's in the casserole."

"Must be an Athena recipe?" Her friend often came up with some creative meatless or extra-vegetable-laden meals for her players that were unorthodox but delicious. Jenny had only tried a few dishes from Athena's first cookbook filled with recipes for athletes, but had loved them all.

Paul's smile was warm. "It is."

Dylan made introductions, then upon hearing the sound of nails clacking quickly against the hardwood floor, Jenny turned. A large black dog's tail thumped through a potted fern, sending leaves flying and fronds swaying. The dog beelined to Dylan at a trot, then landed in a seated position against his legs. It squirmed, then got up and danced around him, giving his leg a quick sniff before sitting again and putting its head up to smile at him.

"How's Fish settling in?" Jenny asked, referring to the rescue dog Brant had convinced Dylan to adopt after a short trial period.

"She's doing really good, isn't she?" Dylan replied in a cute voice and the dog went wilder, if possible. Dylan stood up, crossed his arms, and sternly commanded, "Sit!"

Fish promptly sat on Dylan's feet, leaned back against him, tongue lolling as she looked up at him in adoration, awaiting the next order. Then the dog was back on all fours, dancing. "She's crazy responsive to tone."

"I'll say."

"Sorry," Paul called from the kitchen. "After I picked her up from doggy daycare, I barricaded her in your room so she wouldn't maul the two of you."

"She knows how to break out," Dylan said.

"With the proper motivation, obviously," Paul agreed. "She didn't break out to see me."

Dylan set the dog out where she zipped straight to a patch of grass, throwing herself down and rolling around on her back.

"I've got some trunks and a shirt you can wear in the hot tub if you want. I promise the dog won't join us in the water. Okay, I can only promise that if we lock her inside. She tries to follow me everywhere. I can't tell you how many times I've almost closed a door on her poor nose."

Jenny laughed. The dog was already back at the glass door,

which she now noticed was smeared with nose and tongue prints. "Let's hit the hot tub if I can wear something of yours that isn't a white shirt."

Dylan shook his head but she saw the telltale hint of a smile as she trailed after him into the depths of his modern looking home, wondering who was this man she'd fallen in love with.

* * *

Dylan didn't fully relax until Jenny had sunk into his hot tub, the borrowed blue T-shirt turning black as it grew wet, the fabric billowing around her torso as the jets blasted their limbs.

Jenny sighed, her eyes closing, beautiful with her smile of contentment.

He drifted closer, sitting so his arm rested across the back of the tub behind her. It didn't matter what they were doing, he couldn't seem to get enough of her.

"This is just what I needed," she murmured. "A soak before supper."

"My hot tub is yours any time you need it." He pushed their finished appetizer, nachos with an athlete-friendly version of queso, further from the water's edge.

"A man who has it all," she said, eyes still closed, her head tilted back to the night sky. "If you move out to Sweetheart Creek, you can put this in the backyard." Her smile grew as though imagining the future.

Dylan linked his hand with hers under the water, thinking life didn't get any better than this. Soaking with Jenny and dreaming about their future. The last time he'd visited her, he'd noticed a house a few doors down from her place was for sale. They could move in there, keep an eye on her grandfather, yet still be close to her store and raise their kids in a town where he wouldn't worry if they roamed or played street hockey out front.

On the other hand, if he got traded, it might still all be okay because people who loved each other found ways to make it work. He closed his eyes to the sky, making a silent wish that it would all stay easy and that Miranda would keep him on the roster for at least another season.

"How's the arm?" he asked Jenny as the playlist started a new song.

"Hm?" She opened one eye, her chest and body bobbing in the water, lifting her from the seat as the jets pushed against her back. "Oh, feeling better." She lifted her left arm, squeezing her hand, flexing her elbow. "No more tingles."

"And your knee?"

"Still tender."

She'd ripped the knee out of her jeans, the denim taking most of the damage other than the jarring bruise that had bloomed like a rose over her kneecap.

"Kiss me," he whispered.

Her eyes sparkled as she leaned in for a long kiss.

"I thought for a foolish moment or two this afternoon that you were mad I'd ruined our date," she said.

"Ruined? Never." He caught himself leaning away. He slipped an arm around her, kissing her to remove any doubts that she was exactly where he wanted her. Whole and okay. His.

She lifted her lips from his. "But you seemed upset."

And she'd seemed scared. Scared of the press and his public life—or what it could be if left unmanaged.

"I was worried, Jenny. And angry at the reporters for being such heartless, inhuman—"

She put a finger against his lips, silencing him, preventing his anger from welling like lava up a volcano. "Why worried?"

"That was a bad tumble. And I..." He pushed a wet hand through his hair, his fingers sticking to the dry strands. He pulled his hand away, locks falling over his forehead. Jenny tenderly brushed them away.

"You what?"

He shrugged, not wanting to put words to his fears when everything in this moment seemed fine.

"What, Dylan?"

"I should have protected you better."

"You think I'm not capable of taking care of myself?"

"I—" He closed his mouth, realizing her eyes were twinkling and that she was poking fun at him. Still, both things were true—she could take care of herself and he should have protected her better.

He turned her hand over in his. She shifted in the water, facing him more fully, her leg against his.

"You're a very important part of my life. And I worried the reporters might scare you away. That you'd think that kind of frenzy was normal—which it isn't—and that you might decide I wasn't worth it." He squeezed her hand, swallowing hard, letting out his worst fears. "That *we're* not worth it."

She bit the corner of her lip, fears flitting across her eyes like ghosts. She said bravely, "It'll take a bit more than that to be rid of me."

They were silent for a moment, Jenny facing the opposite end of the tub again. "Do you think they'll hound us?" Her big eyes turned to him. "One of them knew my name."

He considered her question. He'd pushed some reporters

and could get painted as a beast online if anyone captured a shot of it, which they surely had. But it would be on him. Not her. Unless he was a beast protecting her. Which he had been.

"They won't hound you," he said, hoping it was true. He wasn't popular or tainted by speculation and scandal, like Maverick. And he and Jenny weren't a high-profile couple like Miranda and Dak. Honestly, they were pretty boring by comparison.

He sunk deeper into the water, grateful for the way he'd never fit the famous hockey player, rich dude mold, making his personal life somewhat dull to the press and general public. And Jenny was just Jenny. She'd never fit the hockey player girlfriend stereotype, and that should provide extra immunity, right?

Either way, it was a very different conversation than he'd had with his ex-girlfriend, Dana. She'd wanted to run into the kind of chaos they'd experienced today, not away from it. He'd seen what embracing it had led to. Now he'd see what ignoring it did.

"Dylan?"

There was something in Jenny's voice that sent an edge of panic through him.

She turned to him, her eyes serious and mood suddenly somber. "What if we don't have enough in common to make this work long-term?"

He sat up straight, sending water sloshing. "What?"

"I don't know." She shrugged, looking away, as if embarrassed. "What if you get bored sitting on the couch with me when I'm not out there trying to learn a new sport so I can play with you? So we can follow your interests?"

"Where's this coming from? Don't we have fun together no matter what we do?" Just because he was a pro athlete, that didn't mean everything had to be a high-level competition or he wasn't enjoying himself.

"Yeah, but..." She shrugged. "We were just having fun and now..."

Now they were in love. And it had suddenly become very, very real to her. He leaned back against the tub's edge, inhaling, gathering his thoughts and arguments for all the reasons they worked and always would.

"I want to be a part of your life," he told her. "From the everyday to the special. I want to deliver secret Santa stuff with you. I want to share that experience with our kids." A small lump was forming in his throat and he wasn't sure if it was over fear that the future he saw might never come to light, or for some other reason. "I want to take you to my away games and try new restaurants in cities we may never see otherwise. I want to take in matinees when our plane lands early. I want to go to a barn dance to see what it's all about." He sighed, realizing it was true. For Jenny he would wear the tight jeans, learn to two-step and smile while doing it all. "I think there will be very little time on the couch when it comes to you and me."

She was watching him, brow furrowed as though unsure whether to believe him or not.

"And if I do want to go wall climbing or something like that, I'll call up one of the guys. If I want to watch a movie, get shot at, or chase an armadillo then I'll call you."

That earned a half smile. "Yeah, I'm a good time, aren't I?"

"I somehow doubt being with you is just sitting on a couch, Miss Secret Elf."

She smirked, eyes dancing, her fears seemingly shed. "Do you know what Gramps thought I should call the Secret Elf Collective?"

"What?" His arm was still across the back of the tub, and he scooted her closer so they were thigh to thigh.

"The Secret Elves of Xmas."

"Why?"

"The acronym."

Dylan hissed out a laugh, then realizing he was holding back with the one person he never should, he let it out, loud and free. He wiped his eyes, making his face even wetter with his hand, loving Jenny's happy look.

"You have a nice laugh."

"We're the real deal, Jenny. Opposites in some ways maybe, but I think that's what makes us great and interesting."

The tension that had been etched across her face washed away as her sunshine shone through again. "Yeah?"

"We'll never get bored of each other. I promise you that."

She laughed. "Okay."

He slid his pinkie finger through hers like Rylnn had made him do when they were pinkie swearing to something. "Promise?" he whispered.

Jenny giggled, leaning into him. "I promise." She gave him a sweet kiss. "I love you, you know that?"

"Nah, I'm too grumpy. And for the record, grumpy men should not be considered sexy," he said, quoting her.

Jenny gasped. "You heard me and April talking that day you came to the store to ask me out!"

He smiled and swung her through the water and into his lap, her hands landing loosely behind his neck.

"Well," she murmured, "this woman happens to like grumpy. At least your version of it."

"Thank goodness, or I'd be lost and alone."

"I told you when we met," she whispered, her lips hovering above his own, "I'm a keeper." She landed another light kiss he wanted to take deeper, but there was something wrong with her claim.

"You didn't say that at all. You tried to show me all the reasons you weren't for me."

"You need to listen better. I told you I'm independent, own my own business…"

"Hm." He nuzzled her neck. "I do like those qualities."

"See?"

"And I do listen."

"Do you?"

"I know you actually like neck kisses."

"Do I really?"

He nuzzled in, kissing her neck, earning a moan of happiness from the woman he loved. Yes, she definitely loved neck kisses, and he definitely loved his Jenny. Nobody could fill the spaces between his ribs and around his heart in the way that she did. And nobody else ever would.

CHAPTER 13

February had been a crush of practices and games as well as more rehab for his foot. Dylan was glad that he'd booked this Indigo Bay trip for himself and Jenny back in December. They needed it. Even though their getaway was only two and a half days, midweek, wedged between games, it was enough. Time with Jenny.

He knew many of the players were sneaking away to enjoy their couple of days off, but he doubted they were flying from Texas to South Carolina. That meant they'd have the beach town to themselves for their respective birthdays. No distractions or interruptions.

Dylan pedaled slowly behind Jenny, watching her two wheels wobble and weave across the paved beach path littered with sand.

"It's just like riding a bike," she muttered as he drew up alongside her.

"Look ahead, not down." He cringed as Jenny veered toward a palm tree at a curve in the path before yanking herself straight. She inhaled and lifted her chin, the ocean breeze ruffling the tendrils of brown hair that had escaped both her ponytail and her helmet. Her bike immediately straightened out.

"Well, how about that?" She grinned at him, wobbled, then took off at a pace that got his heart pumping as he raced to catch up.

She was wearing an outfit that was a far cry from her usual cowgirl getup and he wondered where on earth she'd found it. She was in a long-sleeve, pale blue top, a pair of sunny yellow capris and matching flip-flops that showed off her shapely ankles.

"You're smiling," she said, daring to peek over at him when he pulled up alongside her pink bicycle again.

"Yeah." He realized it was true. He was happy. The past few weeks had been quiet, no press hounding them, no more worries about how opposite their worlds were. Just happiness. Busyness and happiness.

Now that they were away from it all for a few days, he was already relaxing and his worries over his still bothersome foot felt like they belonged to someone else. That and the prospect of a trade, since he was burning up the ice every time he stepped back onto it. According to the local sports pundits, he was a man renewed and inspired. Age and injury couldn't slow him down.

The proclamation had made him snort and turn off the TV, then slide his bay window's curtain to the side to double-check that his front lawn hadn't filled up with hopeful reporters looking to build him into some sort of superhero because he was still able to play—even though it secretly hurt to keep doing so.

Although Karlene might be figuring it out. She'd poked his foot after a game that had gone into overtime, and he was pretty sure she'd glimpsed the full picture when he'd recoiled and cursed. He much preferred it when she didn't make herself available right after the games.

Dylan puffed as he caught up to Jenny after she'd zipped off again with a joyful squeal. His time on stationary bikes hadn't quite equipped him for the extra work a real bike was. Especially this well-loved rental that could use a new chain and a major tune-up.

"And you were worried that I needed to do stuff with super jocks in order to be happy off the couch?" he muttered, pretending to be put out by the fact that she'd taken off on him.

Jenny shrugged. "You *are* a professional athlete in his prime. I know I slow you down."

"I should wash your mouth out with soap."

She giggled. "Wash it out with ice cream, if you don't mind." She stood on her pedal, pumping hard. "Try and catch me!"

He raced to do just that, though he was slowed down by pedestrians and more leisurely cyclists. The day was gorgeous with waves gently crashing against the shore to their right and the resort's multicolored cottages standing in rows on the left.

When he pulled alongside her again, she was breathing hard, a big smile on her face. "I'm going to need a hot tub tonight. My legs feel like jelly. Did I tell you the inside of my thighs were killing me the day after you taught me to skate?"

"I'll bet. Learning to skate uses a lot of muscles."

They pedaled further, their pace slow and even.

"I could live here," Jenny said, inhaling deeply. "Imagine seeing the ocean every day."

"You'd move?" Would she take her grandfather with her?

Or was she just dreaming and not actually considering leaving Sweetheart Creek? If he got traded, would she come with him? It was the first time she'd ever said something like that with a hint of seriousness in her voice, and it got his hopes up.

"I don't know." Her nose scrunched as she considered his question. "Sweetheart Creek is home."

"That would make it hard to leave."

"Yeah." She turned to him, her expression thoughtful. "Does Wisconsin feel like home to you? You said San Antonio's just a pit-stop."

"I've learned not to get too attached to a place," he said, mulling over the idea of 'home.' To him it was more than just a feeling of familiarity like the old dairy farm where his parents still lived. It was somewhere he felt contented, relaxed, happy and himself.

"Home's not geographical," he said, realizing that he felt contented as well as himself right now, in a strange new town in South Carolina.

"I think home might be anywhere you are, Jenny."

* * *

As the path wove its way past a wedding being set up by the water, Jenny was still smiling over Dylan's proclamation that home was wherever she was. She slowed to take in the beautiful scene. An archway woven with flowers. A few chairs with ribbons. It was a small, intimate affair. Very romantic.

"Who do you think's getting married?" she called to Dylan, who had dropped behind her. "Maybe it's a second marriage? A couple of older folks finding love in their eighties?"

"I overheard staff talking about a hockey player getting married when I checked in."

"Like, NHL?"

"Dunno. But I saw a photographer snooping around."

She felt her stomach tumble at the idea of photographers being on the lookout for a hockey player and then finding her and Dylan. Not that the press ever seemed to go crazy over Dylan. Not even after he'd waded into that crowd of reporters to rescue Daisy-Mae and Miranda. Thankfully, they'd been able to enjoy several weeks of peace since then. But being caught in that media storm, even just the once, had left her slightly on edge.

"Don't worry," Dylan said, the ocean breeze pressing his black athletic tee against the hard planes of his chest. "He saw me and didn't take a single photo."

"Your scowl broke his cameras, did it?" She laughed and he frowned adorably. Every time she saw a photo of him online, he seemed to be scowling, sending out strong 'leave-me-alone' vibes, especially recently.

They continued cycling, enjoying the sea breeze, the gentle burn in their quads and the solidity of the seats under them and the precious balance that kept them upright. As they exited the resort area, they slowed as the foot traffic increased, then turned onto a boardwalk, walking their bikes.

"I'm thirsty. How about you?" Jenny asked, already taking her wallet out of the small bag she had clipped around her waist. She spied a coffee hut just down the pier and began moving toward it.

Moments later she veered off course, distracted by a T-shirt stand selling onesies for babies. She selected one for April's new baby girl who had arrived a few weeks ahead of schedule, just days before the trip, healthy and clearly in charge. Jenny had momentarily considered canceling the Indigo Bay getaway, since April's temporary replacement wasn't due to step in at the store for almost another two weeks. Instead, Jenny, who'd already arranged to have the Gavras sisters—Athena and Meddy—look in on Gramps, had closed her store with barely a second thought and jumped on the plane.

She was already so glad she had, even though it meant a few days of lost income.

"Looks like it might rain," Dylan said as she tucked the tiny garment in her waist sack. He bent his neck back, looking at the gray clouds moving over the darkening water ahead of them.

"I'm waterproof. Latte?"

"Iced coffee for me, please. Decaf. Black." He released his helmet and wiped an arm across his forehead, his gaze taking an admiring sweep down Jenny's calves. She was tempted to pose and angle her foot to give him a better view.

They took their coffees to the edge of the boardwalk's pier, sitting on a bench and gazing out at the coming rain. Streaks of gray connected the clouds to the water below and the breeze off the water turned cooler.

"Thanks for the coffee," Dylan said.

Jenny knocked her cup against his. "To vacations, when and where you can get 'em. Thanks for bringing me here."

"I don't want to go anywhere without you," he said, leaning in to give her a long kiss.

"I love you."

"I love you, too."

Shoulder to shoulder, they knocked their paper cups together again. "To coffee," he said.

"And good company."

Did it get much better than this? Her boyfriend, the beach, an ocean breeze to cool her down after their brisk ride, and coffee.

Someone nearby asked, "May I?"

Jenny turned to see who was talking to them. A man in a black vest with a thousand pockets had a large camera poised at eye level as he waited for them to reply.

She startled. "What?"

"No, thank you," Dylan said firmly, putting out a hand to block the shot.

Jenny heard the telltale sound of a shutter, knowing he'd got the photo before it had been blocked. Then the man made a beeline back to the safety of the boardwalk.

Dylan muttered something in Dutch, then stood, shoulders wide, eyes narrowed. "Let's go."

"Good idea." She shivered and dropped her half-finished coffee in the trash, following him off the pier and boardwalk area.

They biked back toward the resort; the rain catching up with them. The storm's increasing wind pushed at their side and a few drops landed, speckling the asphalt path under their tires.

"Wanna race to the cottage?"

She grinned and lifted her feet off the pedals, sending them out by her sides. "Are you kidding? I love the rain!" She tipped her head back and laughed, her bike wobbling so badly she almost fell.

"You're such a kid," Dylan said affectionately.

"It's why you love me. I'm tough, but I'm really, really fun, too."

They rejoined the trail that led to their resort, peddling over arched bridges and sending birds flying into the air.

Jenny squealed in surprise, then tossed her head back and laughed as the rain grew harder. Before long, it had become a downpour, and her capris were already starting to stick to her skin.

Dylan directed them to a white gazebo overlooking a pond. They dashed inside, dropping their bikes at its steps. The rain slashed the pond's surface and Dylan pulled Jenny into his arms, warming her.

"This is probably already my most memorable vacation," she said, one palm flattened against his chest.

"Definitely." He lowered his lips to hers, kissing her softly.

In that moment, wet and pressed against her boyfriend as the rain fell around them, she couldn't think of anything more romantic.

Within a few minutes the rain let up a little, allowing them to see across the pond. Another gazebo, large and white and identical to theirs, sat perched over the water, the murmurings of a song reaching them.

"There's a band," Dylan said as they stepped to the railing, looking to the other gazebo.

"Frank Sinatra?" she asked, tipping her head to listen.

"I thought good Texan cowgirls only knew country artists?"

"I do love a good Carrie Underwood song. But Frank's in a category all his own."

Dylan held out his hand, the warm dampness of his clothing surrounding her as she stepped into his embrace. They found the beat and rhythm, using the gazebo as their own private dance hall, the rain still falling around the open walls like a curtain. It felt good to be in his arms and she realized that to her, he felt like home, too. When she was with him it was easy to feel content, to feel safe and loved. What had started as a whimsical adventure had become something real.

They moved to the song, then the next as it blended into the first. Jenny snuggled closer, her head resting against Dylan's cheek. "Definitely the most memorable."

The rain slowed, the music slowly growing louder. Finally, the sun came out, their song ended along with the rain. Dylan stepped back, bracing her face with his hands, and kissed her the way she'd always dreamed of being kissed.

They hugged, still swaying as a rainbow formed over the pond, stretching high above them, getting brighter and brighter before melting into the sunny sky.

Jenny sighed. "I love rainbows."

Dylan glanced at the blue sky again, releasing her so they could collect their wet and abandoned bikes. "How about unicorns?"

"Don't forget sprinkles."

"Glitter?"

"I do like my bling. I convinced Daisy-Mae to create a Dragons jersey with some bling for us gals. I hear Rylnn loves hers."

"That was you?" Dylan looked at her as though she'd broken some vital code.

"Daisy-Mae says they're selling like hotcakes."

"The guys are in an uproar. The desecration of our jerseys..." He slowly shook his head. "Our *man*hood."

She smiled and reached across the space between them and their bikes to smooth his unruly hair, standing up wildly from the rain. "It's just a jersey, hon."

He dropped his helmet in the grass. "Just a jersey?" The bike went next as he gave her a very fake looking scowl, his eyes twinkling, hands on his hips as he marched toward her.

Jenny jumped on her bike, laughing as she looked over her shoulder. He caught her before she could even move an inch, pulling her from the bike and into his arms where he proceeded to kiss her without mercy.

* * *

As the dinner cruise's boat docked back in Indigo Bay's harbor, Dylan kissed Jenny's cheek, his arms wrapped tight around her as they watched fireworks flare and explode in the night sky. Dinner had been romantic and lovely. The other couples on board had been caught up in their own worlds and hadn't interrupted them and their birthday dinner.

It made him wonder if this was what his eventual retirement could be like. Within a year or two, nobody would remember him, and the idea of leaving hockey, instead of bothering him, intrigued him. Could he simply move on with life? Create a family, use his business degree to continue to build up his property investments and carry on like a regular Joe?

He'd still miss hockey, he knew that. But maybe not the grueling schedules and time away from the people he loved.

The captain stood on the lit-up dock, welcoming his passengers back to dry land. Dylan exited first, straightening his suit jacket over his yellow Hawaiian shirt before turning to help Jenny in her heeled sandals down the short ramp between the boat and dock. Something flashed and he was momentarily blinded.

Before his eyes could clear the white spots at the center of his vision, Jenny was at his side, ushering them along.

"Was that a photographer?" he asked, trying to catch what was happening by focusing on his peripheral vision.

"Yes."

"Well, he got his shot. Again. Maybe he'll leave us alone now."

They headed back to the resort, taking a ride share. They were let out at the main entrance and they walked along the palm-lined, crushed seashell path lit by tiki torches. It wove past the outdoor restaurant and one of the pools, branching off in various directions to lead to different cottages.

Dylan stopped suddenly. He tugged Jenny back behind the shelter of the path's short palms.

"What?" she whispered, leaning forward to peer around the palm.

"Shh! Is that...?" Dylan squinted, pulling her down into a crouch. Surely his eyes were deceiving him. "Was that Daisy-Mae and Maverick?"

Jenny popped up, then down again, her dark linen skirt puffing up under her. "She's wearing a white dress!"

"You have wedding fever. It's a sundress." He'd noticed the way Jenny had taken an extra-long look at the beach wedding set up earlier that day, just about steering her bike into the sand as she did.

"No, no. It's *more* than that, Dylan!" She shook his arm, her voice filled with excitement. "The hockey player wedding! And you said the other guys on the team were fighting over this trip in the gala's auction in December, and that a bunch of them are sneaking away for trips right now, too!"

"You think..."

Jenny straightened, taking another peek and gasping loudly. Dylan, feeling a rush, hushed her, pulling her back down again by the hem of her white, loose knit cardigan.

"Violet and Leo are here!" She was shaking his arm so hard, he nearly fell over. "Look at Mav's outfit. Look!" Dutifully, he lifted out of his crouch to take another peek. "That's not beach attire. Same with Violet's dress and Leo's suit. Maverick and Daisy-Mae eloped! I'm sure of it."

He lowered himself again, nodding to a couple who were walking past them on the path. "Hey, how are you doing? We just lost a contact lens." He dabbed the ground with a finger. "Oh, there it is."

They gave him and Jenny a strange look, and moved quickly past. He caught Jenny biting back a laugh as the couple fled with one last darted glance.

"Do you think it was their beach wedding we saw being set up?" Jenny asked, her tone hushed, taking another peek around the palm. She frowned suddenly, her head shaking vigorously. "No. That doesn't make any sense. Daisy-Mae thinks elopements are dumb. But this had to have been an elopement."

"Maybe she really is pregnant?" he asked, referring to the latest rumor.

Jenny's mouth dropped open, then she covered it, eyes wide. "You think the reporters are right?"

Dylan shrugged, letting Jenny pop up to spy a moment longer as the two couples left the outdoor restaurant, disappearing down a path that led away from the one they needed to take to their cottage.

He waved Jenny to follow him as he bent over, tiptoeing down the path.

"Come on. Quietly." They veered off the walkway and into the soft sand. Jenny paused to slip out of her shoes and Dylan did the same.

"We can make a break for it." He pointed toward a few nearby cottages that would give them cover as they escaped to their own purple one. There was no way he was going to risk his colleagues seeing them and crashing his getaway with an obligatory drink or whatnot. Jenny—and the precious few hours they had together here—were all his.

They bent over as they raced, trying to stay low as they jogged across the sand. His right foot ached as the shifting grit forced his foot's muscles to bend and flex in ways it normally wouldn't. He wasn't sure if this was good for it, or not.

Breathless, they ran up the steps to their private cottage, Dylan unlocking the door. The seashell wind chime tinkled in the breeze, and a warm gust came off the land toward the ocean behind them.

"Wait." Jenny caught his hand. "Can we sit out here for a bit? It's really nice out."

She tipped her head toward the double hammock set in one of the sand dunes that surrounded the cottage. She barely had to give him an inviting smile and he was tossing his shoes, and hers, into the cottage and closing the door again, leading them back into the quiet night.

"Oo! Ouch." Jenny tiptoed across the rock-lined, crushed seashell path between their little house and the hammock. Dylan swept her into his arms before she could protest, carrying her to the safety of the soft, cool sand on the other side.

He set her down, then climbed into the hammock, steadying it for her so she could crawl in beside him. She snuggled against him, rolling onto her side so her head was on his shoulder, her hand on his stomach. Bliss. Home.

She toyed with the delicate white gold heart necklace he'd bought her for her birthday, gasping softly. "You can see the stars!"

They rocked gently, listening to the sounds of the water, and the odd couple heading home to their own cottage. Jenny pointed out a few constellations, all of them incorrect, clearly proving she knew nothing of astronomy. But the stories she made up to go with them were worth the chatty stream of misinformation.

"Would you elope?" In Dylan's limited experience, he'd noted that women tended to have a firm view of what they did and did not want when it came to their ideal future weddings.

"Sure."

He pretended to sit up, half-serious. "Maybe they're still set up down at the beach and can slip another one in today."

"Don't try to scare me off, silly man." She tugged him down, resting her head against his shoulder again.

He pulled her closer, the quiet whispers of the palm fronds above filling the silence of the night, tucking around them, a hum of contentment vibrating through Dylan like a vital current.

"I should ask to get traded here," he said sleepily.

"You're not getting traded," Jenny murmured. "Ever. I'm going to tell Miranda you have to stay with the Dragons until you're old and gray and can no longer stand up in skates."

"Yeah?"

"Yeah." There was a firmness to her tone, then her head left the warmth of his shoulder, creating an unwelcome cool spot. "Where are the talks at these days?"

He stayed silent a long moment, the contented hum lessening.

"Dylan?"

He inhaled swiftly. "They've intensified." Everyone believed he was healed and as strong as ever. Denver still wanted him back.

He rolled his ankle, stretching his foot, waiting for the familiar ache at the top of his right foot. There it was.

"What?" She sat up, eyes wide in the pale beam from the cottage's porch light.

"Let's not talk about it now."

"But you can say no if you get traded, right? Beg Miranda to keep you? Or Louis? You have a choice, don't you?" He could hear the pain in her voice and he pulled her closer, not wanting to talk about the odds of a trade and spoil this moment.

"Anything can happen at any time. It's the reason I don't often put down roots."

Miranda knew Dylan was happy where he was. And she seemed pleased with how he was playing. Win-win, right? Why change things just because Denver wanted a reunited Double D? He had to believe everything was going to work out for him, and he'd get to stay where he belonged. With the Dragons. With Jenny.

Jenny sat up again, her feet swinging over the side of the hammock. "I just can't..." Her voice choked, the rest of the sentence locked inside her.

Dylan drew her into a tight hug, pulling her back into the hammock. He loved hockey, but he planned to have a lot more future years with Jenny than with the NHL. She was now a factor that weighed heavily into every decision he made. He murmured truthfully, "I'd threaten to quit before I moved away from you."

* * *

Jenny's phone pinged with a notification and she moved around the bed to pick it up. She'd tossed and turned most of the night, unable to discard the idea that Dylan might be forced to move across the country in a trade back to Colorado sooner rather than later. She'd always known it was a possibility, but it had never felt more real than now.

If he got traded, would that be it for them? How could either of them slip away for any significant amount of time if he was on the other side of the continent? She couldn't keep dropping her life in the hands of others—her store, her grandfather—to go spend a few hours with Dylan between games and practices. And it wasn't like he could come see her all the time, either. He'd be in the western division again, meaning his regular season games wouldn't often bring him to her part of the country.

And of course, Miranda would trade him. She was a smart businesswoman. Dylan was a great player, and her team needed money. But it also needed great players.

Jenny pulled her hands down her face, trying to wrestle her mind into finding a solution in an impossible situation.

There wasn't one. The geographical distance, if he moved, would be too great. The strain of making things work without their lives and careers falling apart would be intense. It was already almost too much. And even though Dylan had said he'd threaten to quit before being traded, she knew she'd never come between him and hockey. It wasn't a choice she ever wanted him to have to make. He'd sacrificed much of his life for the game so he could get to this level, and she was just someone he'd loved for a few months. It was no contest. As much as she loved him, and as much as she'd be heartbroken, he needed to choose hockey.

She inhaled, resolved to stop fretting so she didn't ruin the last day of their trip. She'd always known their relationship would end if he got traded, and she was determined to enjoy every last bit of their adventure up until that moment eventually came.

Currently it was still predawn, and they'd planned to watch the sunrise from the hammock, then enjoy a walk down to a little café for lunch before their afternoon flight so Dylan could make his home game.

Jenny lifted her phone, noting that the notification was for a Dylan Spotting. Her heart stuttered. What would it be about? Trade talks? One of the photos that man from yesterday had snagged?

Steadying herself, she opened the notification, preemptively wincing as her imagination ran away with possible headlines, certain her anonymity and love life were about to be shattered.

She closed one eye and peered at her phone.

Last night, during the boat cruise. Dylan was wearing the gag gift Hawaiian shirt she'd got him for his birthday. She hadn't expected him to wear it to supper, but he'd said because she was wearing the gold heart necklace he'd got her, it was only fair he wore his—under his suit jacket. Small gifts from the universe, because that shirt was truly too much on its own.

In the photo, Dylan was helping her off the boat. At least she knew it was her, because she recognized her cardigan sleeve. The rest of her had been cut off, deemed unworthy of interest.

She lowered her phone and considered how she felt.

Relieved. There was nothing to instigate backlash, speculations or invasions of privacy.

But she also felt the deep, echoing sting of hurt and unworthiness. Wasn't she worth being shown off?

She shook off her thoughts. He was at the center of some

trade talks. That was all the hockey world cared about. That was what the world *should* care about.

Without reading beyond the headline stating that Dylan had slipped away for a little R&R between games, she deleted the notification for Dylan's name, then the app itself.

She inhaled again, setting her phone down. At least it wasn't a notification that he'd been traded.

She needed to savor these small moments of gratitude, linking them together to create a good day, a good life, and a beautiful relationship that would last as many days as they were gifted.

She squared her shoulders, grabbed a blanket, and headed out to watch the sunrise with the man of her dreams.

Moments later, she was tucked under two cozy blankets, her limbs wrapped around Dylan.

"You okay?" he asked, as though aware of the tension that had begun to hum in the background after their talk about his trade prospects.

"Hm. Yeah." Jenny snuggled in further.

"I have a string of games starting tonight," Dylan said, rubbing her shoulder, his thumb moving to gently brush her cheek. "I won't get to see you for a few days. Three. Three long days." His voice was husky and he kissed the top of her head, and her eyes dampened. Why couldn't their relationship have stayed as a light and fun adventure? Now the idea of him moving away from her, or even being gone for several days, hurt her heart.

"Why don't you tag along?" he asked, his voice bright with possibility as a streak of pink stretched across the sky.

"I'm sure that's not allowed."

"Hockey wives do it all the time."

"I'm not a hockey wife."

"We could fix that." He lifted her left hand in his right, stroking the bare spot where a ring should be, and her heart galloped at an unsteady pace. "Come with me this week. I'll take care of the plane tickets, hotels, and meals."

Jenny chewed the inside of her cheek, her gaze flitting over the sand dunes, barely noticing the small bird tracking up and down the one beside them as though it had lost something.

Her mind was filled with static.

She loved Dylan.

They'd only been dating a few months.

He was hinting at marriage.

She wanted to say yes. Wanted to jump.

But jumping meant selling her store—her job. Leaving Gramps. Leaving her community, her friends, her home for the past 32 years.

Jumping meant being with Dylan.

But what if…what if this was like her old relationship with Ranger, just version 2.0 with better love bombing blinding her from reality?

She gave herself a mental shake. Dylan wasn't like Ranger. He was genuine. He loved her. Ranger never had.

"It's too soon for marriage," she blurted out.

His hand stopped caressing her shoulder. "Okay."

"Sorry," she muttered.

"Would you come on the road with me this week?" His tone was tentative. "Give it a try?"

"I can't."

"How come? What do you need?"

"You'll be working and so should I. April's replacement doesn't start for almost two weeks. We trained her over the past several weekends, but she still has to finish up her other job before she can move full-time to Blue Tumbleweed."

The scheduling of the new shop assistant had been tight and strictly based on April making it very close to her due date. She hadn't, which meant Jenny needed to be in her store every day for at least the next month. The first two weeks, so her doors could stay open and she could earn a living. The second two weeks, so she could make sure her trainee had a firm grip on the reins before Jenny took any time off.

"You don't want to tag along and fawn over my stardom?" he joked, referencing their Thanksgiving conversation.

"Funny," she said dryly. She sat up, legs over the side. "But I don't live in a dream world, Dylan. I have a store and employees and a life and a grandfather and chickens and a cat who all need me. Obligations."

"I know you do, Jenny." His voice was soft, tentative, and caring.

Suddenly her life weighed so heavily on her, she wanted to cry. She wanted to follow Dylan and be excited about being with him and seeing new things. She wanted that rush for however long it lasted.

"I can't just go live in your world without my own falling apart. I can't walk away or ignore my responsibilities because you asked me to. Even if I want to."

"We can figure it out."

"But how? This is how it is." She stood, suddenly angry. If she followed him and ignored her own responsibilities, she'd have nothing left to come back to. He might have a household manager who took care of his bills and cut the lawn when he went out. She didn't have that luxury. She'd had to cook and freeze meals for Gramps before coming here so he didn't just eat canned soup the whole time. And her income was going to take a hit this month due to closing her store for three days, midweek. She couldn't even do it for a few more days this month, even though she didn't have an employee to pay over the next two weeks. But as an employer, she did have maternity benefits to pay into because she was a good, kind person who dearly loved her friend and her new baby girl.

The bottom line was that she hadn't just packed her suitcase and walked out the door like Dylan undoubtedly had. And she couldn't just keep walking out of her life over and over again. Even to be with the man she loved.

Dylan's expression was quiet, closed. "What do you need from me? How can I help?"

"You can't, Dylan. That's the thing." They were two people from opposite worlds, and those two worlds were starting to collide in a way that just didn't fully mesh.

"We're here now." She reached for his hand. "Let's just enjoy our last few hours, okay?" His tone was even as he said, "What you said at Thanksgiving is the truth, isn't it? You're not willing to bend your life around mine. At all."

She sighed with her whole body. "I am, Dylan, and I have. I'm here, aren't I? But I can't do it forever without going broke. And Gramps needs someone. He needs me and I can't just ditch or ask my friends to look in on him indefinitely. They have their own lives, too."

Dylan stood, his frustration as clear as her own.

"I'm sorry," she said, "I know it's not fair."

He nodded, the muscle in his jaw flexing. He looked so hurt, she longed to reach out and touch him.

"We have weekends and evenings," she said gently.

"That's when *I* work."

They stared at each other for a long moment.

"I told you at Thanksgiving that spending time together is important to me," he said.

"And I told you that I won't give up my life, my *everything*, for someone else. I owe it to myself to protect what I've built."

"Then what happens to us?"

"I don't know." She covered her face, fighting tears. "I love you, Dylan. So much."

His arms wrapped around her and she sobbed into his chest.

"I just can't see a solution without one of us making a really big sacrifice and losing everything we've worked for." Her life felt suppressing sometimes, but it was her life. If she walked away from it or moved away, what did she have left?

And she wasn't going to become a hockey wife who followed Dylan to games because that wasn't who she was. And she wasn't going to ask him to retire or give up a deal that would be good for his career.

She longed to say yes to him. To just close her eyes and jump, leave her own world and life behind. She was so close. So close. But she couldn't do that to Gramps. Not even if she sold her store and begged him to come along with her.

"We'll figure it out," Dylan said, rubbing her back.

"But we're both burning out with driving back and forth all the time. Mostly *you* driving back and forth because I can't slip away long enough." She sniffed into his cozy sweater, her favorite one of his that made her want to cuddle in and never leave. Life felt so terribly unfair. Why give her a man who was shaping up to be the love of her life if she had to sacrifice everything in order to have him?

"I love you, Dylan." Her voice wobbled. "But you need and deserve more than I can give you."

CHAPTER 14

Dylan paced the cottage, waiting for their breakfast to arrive, trying to find a solution to their relationship problems. Jenny was right. She couldn't just cut and run and it was unfair of him to ask that of her.

He could pay someone to take charge of her store, but he knew she'd never let him do that.

He could hire a nurse to watch out for Garfield, but he knew Jenny loved being with her grandfather and could never just leave him behind. Not for longer than a few nights.

"Dylan?" Jenny's hands shook as she entered the cottage, her phone in hand. She'd stepped out to take a call only moments ago.

He glanced up from his spot by the fireplace, his thoughts still whirling. The look on her face broke his already hurting heart and he covered the space between them in a flash.

"What's wrong?"

"I need to change my flight." Her voice wavered. "Gramps fell and…"

Dylan picked up the cottage's house phone, putting it to his ear.

"What are you doing?" she asked, an edge to her voice.

Taking care of the one thing he could. "Yes, concierge please." He waited for the telltale click of the transferred call, then the crisp reply from the concierge desk. "Yes, this is Dylan O'Neill from the purple cottage. I'm going to need a car to the airport and someone to change two flights for me ASAP. I also need to cancel our breakfast unless it'll be here in less than two minutes."

"Is there a problem, sir?"

"No, it's a family emergency."

Assured the resort's team was on it, he hung up, facing Jenny. "I don't care where we are and what we're doing. If I can be with you, that's where I want to be. Always. And if I can help or do something, I will."

"But…" She blinked, seemingly stunned at his actions.

He pulled her into a giant hug.

"I love you. You and Garfield need me, and I will be here for you. Always."

* * *

People streamed past Jenny in the San Antonio airport, drawling Texan accents reminding her she was home. Home.

Gramps.

In a daze, she moved toward a black sedan with a driver holding up a sign with her name on it.

Then she was inside, buildings blurring past her, then pastures and finally the familiar sights of Sweetheart Creek.

Dylan was on a separate, later flight. He'd put her on the first one, taking her suitcase along with his so she wouldn't have to wait at the baggage carousel. He'd arranged everything. Thought of every detail.

She blinked back tears, thinking how they couldn't last forever—not as a full and complete relationship like they both wanted, where they had free access to each other at any time. And she saw how important that was. She saw her parents doing that with their consulting travel. Always together. And yet they'd sacrificed everything back in Sweetheart Creek in order to have that. They were missing out on their grandchildren, her brothers, herself, and being there for Gramps in moments like this when he'd fallen and needed help.

But her parents had enjoyed the solidity of a decade-long marriage before they'd lifted off and followed her dad's work, her mom training in the same field so they could tag-team contracts.

With Dylan, it felt like she was now hedging her bets, waiting for his trade, waiting for them to fail.

She'd never felt this way about someone before, but she knew both she and Dylan deserved more than they could currently eke out. She had roots here, but would they dry up if she spent some time elsewhere? Her parents were able to come and go. They missed out on a lot, definitely, but they hadn't been completely erased from the town and its history.

The car stopped and she leapt out, her thoughts only on Gramps. She ran up the front walkway and straight into the house.

Just hours ago, he'd called, asking if she could swing by and help him up. He'd fallen down the back steps. She'd scrambled out a question, she couldn't even recall what it had been, but his reply had been a curt, I'm fine. She hadn't had a chance to badger him before she caught telltale, awful retching sounds and he'd hung up. Not fine. A concussion. Brain injury. Her Gramps.

She'd immediately called friends and family, begging them to go check in on him, then she'd been on a flight, out of contact. Not that Gramps had picked up his phone for her at all anyway.

Texts had flooded in when she'd taken her phone off airplane mode, her tiny plane not having in-flight WiFi.

Nothing from Gramps. But Athena had texted.

He's okay. Don't hurry back.

How could he be okay? The steps he'd fallen down were concrete. They were no match for a once-broken, eighty-year-old hip. And he'd *vomited*.

"Gramps!" she called into the house, racing through the rooms. "Where are you? Gramps?"

"In here. Not dead yet!" Thank goodness he sounded cheery. She breathed out a sigh of relief until she heard the sound of his stomach emptying.

Jenny sprinted to the bathroom where he was on his knees over the toilet, alone.

"Didn't Athena stay with you?"

"She's filming recipes with that hockey player of hers. That Chadwick Mullens fella."

"She's *what?*" Those two were sworn enemies the last she'd heard.

"Her cooking channel. She had to hurry back."

"And she just *left* you?"

Earlier, Jenny had almost convinced herself she could run away with Dylan and that her friends would have her back.

"Meddy took over. She ran out to grab something for my stomach."

"Wait. I thought you fell?" He looked green, pale, and had a line of sweat along his forehead.

"I did that, too." He shifted onto his butt, leaning against the tub, clearly exhausted. "Been a busy day." He hoisted a pant leg, showing her an expertly bandaged shin. "Fell down the back steps trying not to throw up on them. Easier to clean up if it's in the grass, you know. But I'm okay."

"I thought you needed help to get up?"

"My leg felt weird and didn't act right for a bit there, but it's alright. I got up before anyone could get here. A man's more afraid of a bad fall than a heart attack at my age."

"So you're okay? What did the doctor say?"

He frowned at her. "I don't need a doctor."

"Gramps! You have a concussion." She paused, taking in his green complexion, "Don't you? What about a hip or leg fracture? How did you fall? You forgot I was away. You hung up on me."

"Sorry for that. I'm gonna need a new phone."

"What?"

"I dropped it. It suffered worse than I did."

"Yeah, but…" She gestured to his leg, his head, all of him, trying to sort out what had really happened and if he was really and truly okay.

"It's the flu, Jenny."

"Are you sure?"

"Very."

She stared at him for a long moment, trying to calm all the questions rocketing through her brain. Finally, she slid an arm under his. "Come on then, let's get you situated somewhere more friendly for your old bones."

"Up we go," he said, straining as he stood.

She got him into his bedroom, propping him up with

pillows. She kept one skeptical eye on him while she grabbed the bathroom's wastebasket, setting it beside him. Was he really okay? Just scraped up and suffering from the flu? Had she overreacted?

She sat on the edge of the bed, watching him. "There's something going around. Both Cass and Landon had it." Her friend was working toward opening her own wedding center outside of town while nannying Landon's girl, as well as taking care of her own son. She was making it work being with an NHLer.

In fact, she was making it look easy. Violet was, too. Daisy-Mae, not so much.

Jenny rubbed her forehead, clearing away the cobwebs of panic that had encased her brain and had kept her from acting rationally for hours. Thank goodness Dylan had taken over or she might be still spinning her wheels and panicking in Indigo Bay.

"Wait. They were sick in December. Is it really the end of February already?" She looked at Gramps. "I've been sucked into my own world, haven't I?"

"Busy falling in love, I reckon," he said, closing his eyes and leaning into the pillows. "Sorry you had to come back early for me."

"What's a few hours?" She let out an involuntary sigh. A few hours might have led to her and Dylan figuring out a way to meld their lives.

Oh, who was she kidding? It wasn't going to work unless one of them let their own lives take a backseat, or they downgraded their relationship to very casual. And casual didn't seem to be a speed in either of their relationship's transmissions.

"What were you doing outside? Why did you fall?"

"Oh, I was in the kitchen looking for ginger ale." He opened his eyes, perking up at the chance to weave a tale. "Athena brought me a few cans this morning when I said I felt a bit sketchy in the ol' tum-tum. So I went in and found one. I was opening one when I felt breakfast coming up for a second look." He gave her a meaningful glance. "Back door was right there so I rushed out, but that dang chicken was out again. I scared what little brains it has straight on out of its head. It squawked and kicked up a fuss and flew up at me. I tried to knock it away while I was trying to get to the lawn and I took the express lane straight down."

"I'm cooking up that chicken tonight," Jenny muttered, shaking her head.

"Yoohoo!" A woman trilled, the sound of the door closing behind her. "Just me!"

"Who's that?" Jenny asked, standing to meet a very vibrant and lively looking woman with white hair and wearing a hot pink jogging suit. Emily? The new neighbor from across the way? The woman who steamed her broccoli according to Gramps and his binoculars?

"You must be Jenny. Good to see you, dear." Emily gave Jenny a quick hug, then brushed past her, making a beeline for the bed with a bag of ice wrapped in a towel. "I got ice for your leg. Has Meddy come back with something stronger than ginger ale to help settle your stomach, honey?"

The woman propped Gramp's leg on a pillow, then rolled up his pant leg. She methodically placed the ice over his bandage, acting as if she'd raised and nursed a full family of boys. But most remarkable was that Gramps was allowing all of her fussing.

"I can't believe my first aid ice pack was a dud." The woman tutted, picking up a break-and-shake ice pack resting beside a large first aid kit. She tossed it in the bedroom's white wicker trash can, then perched on the edge of the bed. "Now. How's my patient feeling?"

Gramps smiled. "Much better."

She squeezed his hand. "That's what I like to hear, Garfield."

"Sorry, what happened?" Jenny asked, trying to sort out how Emily had become involved. Did Gramps have an extensive support system she'd been unaware of? One that went well beyond her?

"He called me up, asking if I'd ever picked up an eighty-year-old man, and would I like to try today." Emily laughed. "I thought he was asking me out. Finally. But he was on his feet by the time I hightailed it over and then I slowly realized he only wanted me for my retired nursing skills." She gave Gramps a stern look.

He grinned. "Now that I know you're game, when I'm feeling better I'll take you out on the town."

"Promise?"

"I do."

"Then that's good enough for me, hon." She turned to Jenny. "You okay, or would you like me to stay?"

"I've got him. Thank you. I appreciate you coming over."

Emily winked at Gramps like they shared a secret. "I always have eyes on my Garfield."

She gave a little wave and disappeared.

Jenny turned to Gramps as soon as she heard the front door close. "What did *that* mean?"

He gave her a half smile, eyes closed. "Her steamed broccoli ain't half bad."

* * *

Dylan gripped the bag from the pharmacy, set down Jenny's suitcase and rang her grandfather's doorbell. He had an hour before he had to be back on the road to the city for tonight's game. He'd learned a long time ago to always keep a suit with him while traveling, and especially when cutting it close with travel and games. He was expected to show up on game day, fully decked out.

Naturally, he'd brought a suit with him to Indigo Bay and had changed into it in the airport before boarding his flight. Any time he could save a minute today was golden.

He held up the white paper bag when she answered, looking way less panicked than he'd seen her a few hours ago. "I saw Meddy in the shop getting stuff for your grandpa while I was picking up some things."

"You know Meddy?"

"Of course. She hangs around the arena sometimes. She called me while I was on the road. She asked me to bring this over for you. I hope that's okay. You weren't answering your texts or calls. I also added a few things to Emily's original order."

"Emily was there, too?"

"No, sounds like she gave Meddy a list."

Jenny rubbed her eyes, looking exhausted. She picked up her purse from where it rested on the floor, just inside the door. She frowned at her lock screen, then said, "Sorry, I ditched my phone as soon as I got here. I should have let you know I arrived."

He nodded, not mentioning he'd had his hands-free device check his phone for missed messages approximately every thirty seconds between the airport and Sweetheart Creek.

"Garfield's okay?" He'd heard the full story from Meddy. The fall. The flu. But he wanted to hear it from Jenny.

Jenny nodded as her grandfather called out, "Who's there?"

"Hang on!" Jenny pulled Dylan toward the bedroom. "Sorry, I overreacted. I hope changing our return flights didn't cost you too much."

Dylan gave her hand a squeeze, then stopped in the bedroom doorway, saying to Garfield, "I hope your favorite flavor is orange."

The man, his face as pale as his white hair, propped himself higher in the piled-up pillows. "It'll do. What did Emily order up for this sorry old oaf?"

Dylan lifted the bag, unpacking it for Garfield. "She figured you could use some electrolytes." He smiled. "I also added in some orange popsicles for when your appetite starts to come back. And because I wasn't totally sure what we were dealing with, I got you a beanbag heating or cooling bag. It can be heated or chilled. Freeze it or microwave it. Half the team swears by these."

"I've got ice." Garfield gestured to his leg. "Emily played nurse." He waggled his bushy eyebrows, obviously doing much better than he'd led Jenny to believe during his abrupt phone call.

Honestly, it kind of made Dylan angry. The man was an adult with a support system, and his granddaughter felt like she had to drop everything to be there for him.

It was good. Wonderful, in fact. For Garfield.

But as someone who wanted to be important in Jenny's world, too, it also really ticked him off.

The room was silent for an awkward beat.

"Need anything?" Dylan asked.

"Pie?" Garfield asked hopefully. "Once I recover, I'll need to build strength, and there's nothing like one of Paul's apple pies for that."

"I'll see what I can do," Dylan said.

Garfield studied Jenny for a long moment, then Dylan. Finally, he waved at the two of them. "You two go fix whatever your problem is. I'm sorry for whatever part I caused. Now go on and git!"

The two dutifully left the room, and Jenny, seemingly seeing Dylan for the first time, gasped. "You have a game tonight! You have to go!" She began pushing him toward the door, her hands on his chest feeling like drops of rain on the cracked desert ground.

"No, not yet. I have time."

She slowed her pushing, her voice small. "You can't miss hockey."

"I was thinking on the plane," he said, stopping. "We're both in our thirties and not married. We both think our lives shouldn't change just because we found someone amazing. You know?"

She gave him a considering look. "I thought I wanted a man who'd just slip into my life without ripples. Why? So it can be boring?" Her voice raised along with her arms. "I want a man who makes me feel alive, who changes me and my boring old, stuffy small town life! I want ripples! I want waves and tsunamis."

"Tsunamis are scary."

"*This* is scary." She grabbed his hand, holding on tightly. "We've been in the fast lane since we met. It's like my hair is blowing wildly in the wind, exhilaration pumping through my veins at every moment." She looked it too—exhilarated and scared. No, terrified. "I'm so scared I'll lose you."

"Because I might be traded?" he said, confirming what he already knew. She nodded. "You know I want you to come with me wherever I go?"

"Yes. And I want to."

He smiled. He was glad about that.

"How do we make this work?" he asked.

"I don't know."

"I've been greedy," he admitted. "I want it all." Her bangs were getting long and he brushed a strand from her eyes. Her and hockey. A public career, but a private life. The city, the small town. Travel, but being home. Finding home.

She leaned away, her eyes wet, her voice sounding stuffy. "I've been the greedy one! And stubborn."

"You shouldn't have to give up your own story, Jenny. Your town, your community." He lowered his voice. "Your family."

He felt so old and tired in this moment, his foot aching as though in sympathy or to back him up, he wasn't sure which. He was so exhausted from running, pushing, straining, and achieving. Pretending. Pretending he didn't hurt...pretending he wasn't lonely. When he was with Jenny, he could just simply be. Be himself, be relaxed, be happy. He didn't always have to be looking ahead, planning the next day, the next meal, the next big goal.

"You said I deserve and need more," he said softly, "but I think you need it even more. You need more than I've been giving you."

She firmly shook her head. "No, you've been giving way more than I have, making it all work."

"You said it though. You have obligations. I just have hockey. It's easier for me to run out here. I'm willing to take us as far as we can go. And I know it wouldn't work for you to follow me to all of my games. Trying to make life on the road something that could work for us is a silly idea. It wouldn't be us, and it definitely wouldn't be you. I got caught up in a dream that's not ours. I got greedy for you because all I know is that I want you in my life. You don't need to be the footnote in my story. You've got your own story to write."

"What are you saying, Dylan?" Her tone was serious, almost sad and he realized he sounded like he was breaking up with her.

"I'm going to fight for you. For us." Her face relaxed. "We don't have to figure it all out today. Just marry me by summer, okay?"

She laughed, sudden tears streaking down her cheeks. She rolled up on her toes in her uncharacteristic flip-flops, fisted his suit jacket and kissed him with a strength and passion that let him know she still loved him. That she was willing to fight, too.

CHAPTER 15

"What is he doing in there?" Jenny asked Dylan as they waited outside the San Antonio movie theater's restroom for her grandfather. He'd managed to stay awake through the entire movie without nodding off, but now she was wondering if he'd fallen asleep in there.

"I'm sure he's fine," Emily said, joining them from her own trip to the ladies' room.

Emily and Gramps had been dating since his fall at the end of February and things seemed to be going well. So well, in fact, that Jenny had been able to join Dylan for a few away games near the end of their season in April. It had been a blast, but she already understood how travel had lost a bit of its charm for Dylan. Both times their schedules had been precise and full. Even so, they'd managed to sneak in some fun away from the hotel and arena.

Whatever it looked like, she was ready for more adventure. She was also ready for more freedom. She wasn't prepared to leave Sweetheart Creek, at least not fully. But she had some irons in the fire to help her go on more adventures with

Dylan. And she had the perfect one in mind. She just had to find a way to tell him.

"I'm going to get some popcorn for the road," Emily said, zipping off to the concession, leaving Dylan and Jenny standing outside the large theater's restrooms.

"Can you check on Gramps?" Jenny asked Dylan. "See if he fell in or something?"

"He didn't fall in the toilet," Dylan said with a hint of humor. "I'm sure he's fine." Dylan turned to her, expression serious. "And actually, there's something I want to talk about."

"What?" She slipped her arms around his waist. "You want to talk about how much you love me?"

"It's about hockey."

Jenny stilled. It was May, barely a month into the off season. The trade talks had cooled and she'd assumed they'd have all summer, probably well into September or October before they resumed.

The two of them were still wearing out the highway between his place and hers, still figuring things out, taking their relationship a week at a time so she didn't melt down over the uncertainness of their future.

"How soon do you want to have kids?" Dylan asked.

She choked on a breath. Why had his seriousness been replaced with casualness as he leaned against the wall outside the restroom?

"Um. Soon I suppose. What's this have to do with hockey?" Other than the fact that it would be tricky to build a family if he was on the road or living in Colorado.

But she was thirty-two now, and her fertility window wasn't going to stay open forever. It was an important conversation to have, even if they weren't engaged or married.

"So how about I retire and we make things happen?" He pivoted on his shoulder so he was facing her.

Jenny sputtered in surprise. "What? Kids? Now?"

"I'm thinking marriage first. A house we both live in the whole time. A bit of travel. Maybe Spain, Thailand, Australia. A cruise. Then have some kids and add a few more pets from Brant's rescue shelter."

"You're going to retire? Now?" She blinked at him, unable to process what he was saying. They hadn't even discussed him retiring. At least, not outside of the odd theoretical conversation about what he'd do when he did and what it would be like.

"But...you love hockey." She couldn't think of any other argument except for his love of the game and the sacrifices he'd made to get to where he was. Sure, he'd confessed his foot hurt in his skates and it wasn't getting any better. He'd tried a different brand of skate, padding, more PT, everything. It bothered him, but he continued to perform well enough that Denver still wanted him. He couldn't quit because of her. She had a plan. A way to make things work until he was ready to leave the game.

"Hockey's still great," Dylan said. "But there are other things I'd like to do with my life, and I don't want to miss the chance to do them."

"You have time."

"I want to wake up with you every morning, Jenny."

She tried to focus on what he was saying, and what it would look like if he did retire.

"But where would we live?" she whispered, fearing that he'd say Wisconsin or the Netherlands, Denver, or pretty much anywhere far away from Gramps.

"The house down the street from the sugar cookie country

house is still for sale." She loved that he now referred to Gramps' house by her nickname. "It needs a lot of work and could use a few rooms added onto it for our little hockey team, but it has potential and the rumor is that the Kidmans are willing to negotiate."

Jenny laughed. "*Our* little hockey team? I'm not sure I actually agreed to that."

"Come on,"—he winked at her—"a couple sets of twins and we'll be set."

She shook her head in amusement, taking a beat to focus, to soak in and imagine what he was proposing.

A future. For them and their family in Sweetheart Creek.

She was so down for that plan that he probably hadn't even truly needed to ask. He could have just walked her down the street to the Kidman's old place and said 'we live here now' and she would have nodded in agreement.

She crossed her arms so she wouldn't throw herself at him, pretending there were finer points to hammer out before she agreed. "Will Paul come live with us?"

Dylan shook his head at her playful question, the skin around his eyes crinkling.

"What? He spoils me. And Gramps."

"He's just happy he found someone to eat his baking." Dylan patted his flat stomach. "But if I retire, I can join in without Athena killing me."

Jenny laughed. "There's a good reason for retirement."

"Paul's open to a move."

"You've asked?"

"I've floated the idea past him."

"But are you sure? Are you really ready to retire?"

He nodded and she studied his face, finding nothing but certainty.

"No regrets?" she whispered.

"I don't regret fighting my trade."

"The trade to be sent to the Dragons?"

"No, the one back to Denver."

"What? You were going to be traded?" Her heart dropped.

"I told Miranda I was in love and so she couldn't trade me. She agreed."

"She did?" Jenny laughed. There had to have been a lot more to that conversation, but she did like this version. Nevertheless, whatever transpired in reality, she made a mental note to send Miranda a gift basket or to set it up so she got a complimentary outfit the next time she came into Blue Tumbleweed. "I don't understand, though. Isn't Denver still asking after you?"

He nodded.

"Wait. You're not being traded. You..." The truth sunk all the way in. He'd refused to leave the Dragons because he'd refused to leave her. And now he was possibly planning retirement so they could build a life together.

She'd known Dylan loved her, but this was so far above and beyond anything she'd ever expected or could have even dreamed of asking.

She shook her head, knowing that him retiring wasn't the move to make right now. She had things up her own sleeve and she wouldn't let him sacrifice his entire career for their relationship. "You love hockey. You can't leave."

His one eye winced closed. "I signed my retirement papers this morning. It'll be announced tomorrow."

The room spun. He'd quit hockey?

What if he got bored? What if he realized he didn't love her more than the sport? The sport that had been his family and community for so long?

Then she started laughing, unable to stop.

"What?"

"You quit. For me." Her giggles turned into hiccups.

"Yeah. What's wrong? You're not going to break up with me or something, are you?"

She stared at him for a long moment, controlling her laughter. "Dylan," she said soberly, "I also have something to tell you." She grasped his hands in hers, laughter and love bubbling inside her. "I sold my store to April."

He gave her a slow blink. "You sold your store?"

She nodded. "So I could move to San Antonio and become a hockey wife."

He stared at her for a long, long moment. His voice was barely a whisper as he said, "But I retired so I could move to Sweetheart Creek and become your house husband."

She giggled again at the absurdity of it all.

"Well, Paul would do most of that house stuff," Dylan admitted. He stared at her in stunned silence for a moment. "But I was going to bring you coffee at work so you didn't have to drink the diner guck. And organize your Secret Santa stuff for you."

"We really need to communicate more."

He turned so his shoulder blades were to the wall, then sagged into it, pushing a hand through his longish hair. "Yeah. I'll say."

Jenny echoed his pose. "Now what?"

No store. No hockey.

Gramps had a girlfriend who was more than happy to check in on him—in fact, the two of them had been crossing the street to see each other several times a day.

"We get married," Dylan said decisively.

"June?" she suggested, knowing that next month was

ridiculously early, but not wanting to wait. The universe had cleared their plates, giving them the time and space to dive into their relationship in the ways they'd wished for.

"The last Saturday in June," he replied.

"Done." Then she gasped, turning to him. "No! I have it. The fourth of July. Independence Day."

He frowned as she stared at him with meaning. "I don't get it."

"Okay, so it's an excuse for a big party. We were both acting all independent and still are." She elbowed him. "I can't believe you retired without telling me."

"You sold your store!"

"Some people around town still think we hate each other because of last Thanksgiving and the way we sorta fought."

"It wasn't a fight."

"*We* know that. But the thing is, they don't and we've actually been pretty quiet about our relationship. So when we send out the invites, people won't know if it's just a Fourth of July cookout or an actual wedding."

Dylan was frowning, confused.

"Never mind. Stupid idea. Let's just do the last Saturday in June. Lots of people must have figured out we're together by now."

"No, I like it." He took her hand, giving it a squeeze. "We could have fun with that."

"So the fourth?"

He nodded.

Gramps came out of the restroom and Emily returned with a massive tub of popcorn. "Everyone ready?" she asked.

"We're getting married," Jenny announced. "July Fourth."

"Lovely," Emily said. "Congratulations."

"I didn't realize you'd proposed," Gramps asked Dylan, his bushy white eyebrows lowering over his eyes.

Jenny and Dylan shared a look. They both muttered, "Uh."

"Well, let's see the ring," Emily said.

"Yeah...um." Jenny held out her bare finger. "We didn't do that."

"I'll get on that," Dylan said.

"Did you just propose now?" Emily asked.

"We didn't actually do that, either," Jenny said hesitantly.

Gramps chuckled. "Knew this fella was the one for you."

Jenny met Dylan's eyes. "Yeah, me too."

* * *

Dylan heard Jenny open the front door to his San Antonio townhouse, the closing date for their place down the street from Garfield's little country house still not for another few weeks.

His dog Fish leapt up from where she'd been sleeping on his feet in the living room. She barked with such sudden authority that Dylan spilled his sweet tea down the front of his 'I'm a Dragon' T-shirt. He'd been given a lot of merchandise during his retirement party and it seemed a shame not to make good use of it, even though he was technically a former Dragon now.

The dog ran to the door, wiping out as she rounded the bend between the couch and the hall. She barked loudly until she heard Jenny's voice. Then all Dylan could hear was the dog's tail whacking the wall as she greeted his fiancée with enthusiasm.

"How does that not hurt?" Dylan asked, coming up behind the dog as her tail gave a particularly hard thump. "Fish, leave it. Come." He slapped the side of his leg and reluctantly the dog gave up sniffing Jenny's pant legs.

"I got the invitations!" Jenny waved a box in front of him, her eyes dancing with joy. "They're a hoot. People are going to be so confused."

One month until the wedding. It was all terribly fun as well as short notice. He wished he'd be able to see everyone's faces when they received their invitations and tried to figure out what was going on.

Dylan gave Jenny a kiss, then led the way to the kitchen. "Come show me."

She set the box on the black granite counter, opening it. Inside was a thick stack of simple, elegant invites with no wasteful ribbons or beads. He'd given her his top three picks, and she'd chosen his first one.

"Very un-blinged out." He held one up for inspection. "I'm impressed with your restraint."

"It was so hard. But I didn't want them to look too weddingish and spoil the confusion we're trying to create."

Dylan chuckled. Jenny had gotten fully behind trying to surprise their family and friends. A few people knew they were engaged, such as his parents, her parents, and Gramps and Emily. But other than that, it had all been fairly secretive. Jenny didn't even have an engagement ring yet, insisting they needed to wait in case someone busted them while shopping.

As he studied the invitation, he imagined what his impression would be. It did look like a party invite. The invitations read: Come celebrate July 4 with Jenny Oliver and Dylan O'Neill at Peppermint Lodge! A cookout for all ages. All food and chairs will be provided. Please RSVP by June 21 and help us celebrate our new beginning. Our special ceremony starts at 4 PM. Cookout and dance to follow.

He tapped the invite, knowing that 'special ceremony' was ambiguous enough to cause confusion or be disregarded. "Subtle."

Jenny danced, giving an excited squeal.

"We need to get you a ring." Dylan snatched Jenny's hand, stilling her. He ran a thumb over the bare spot where at least one ring should already be sitting.

"People are going to lose their minds," Jenny said, leaning a hip against the counter.

"Do you think people will be surprised?"

April had been sworn to secrecy about their relationship and upcoming wedding, but he'd also been in town regularly, helping Jenny and April with the store. It wouldn't be long before people figured it out. Especially once the invites went out.

Currently, April came in a few hours each day so the two women could go through things on the computer, Jenny bringing her up to speed on the areas she hadn't learned as the store's assistant. Dylan had mostly helped out by holding April's baby girl while they worked, stirring his own desire to start their own little hockey team.

Naturally, Fish was happy to have him to herself all day, and loved being walked early in the morning before the sun got too hot, and then again when it cooled off.

Dylan tucked Jenny against him, giving her a sensual kiss. Joy radiated from her as they parted. "This wedding is going to be so fun. When should we send these out? Give everyone two weeks' notice, or a full month?"

"The shorter the timeline, the shorter the guest list as they'll have made other plans."

She gave him a playful swat.

"They're going to think it's a joke," Dylan said. "Will anyone even RSVP?"

"For a party at the Peppermint Lodge? The new home of NHL superstar goalie Landon Jackson?" She gave Dylan a look. "They'll be clamoring to come. Especially since a little bird told me there will be another NHLer getting married there in the fall before you-know-who goes to training camp."

Dylan shook his head, more interested in his upcoming wedding than his former teammates. "This is what I was working on." Dylan grabbed the ring catalogue he'd been studying before she arrived. "I circled the sets I like."

She began flipping through pages, stopping at the first set, his favorite so far. "These."

"Yeah?"

"Yeah."

"Then let's order them and get them sized." He came up behind Jenny, sliding his arms around her middle and holding her close.

"People are going to think we're in the family way," she said. "Getting married so quickly."

"Maybe we soon will be."

"Don't we want to travel a bit first?"

"How about we start trying by this time next year?"

"Or sooner if we get bored of traveling the world?"

"Okay. And I vote we take a cruise on our honeymoon—I emailed you my top five destination choices."

"Are all of them Spain?"

"Three of five," he admitted. "So we travel and have fun, renovate our house and then when we're done, we have a family."

She turned in his arms so she could face him. "Okay."

He nuzzled her neck, giving her one of those sweet kisses

she seemed to like. "Or we can start trying on our wedding night. Speed up that itinerary a bit?"

She giggled, melting into him.

His heart swelled. He was so darn lucky. The luckiest man he knew. Traded to a struggling new team, broke his foot, and suddenly had the love of his life and a renewed purpose.

He pulled his source of joy back into his arms, giving her another kiss. This latest adventure was starting to look like the best one yet.

The End

ACKNOWLEDGMENTS

This book took me a long time, and at one point I considered simply making this series six books instead of seven to save me the pain of figuring out Jenny and Dylan's story. Instead, I kept writing, hoping the story would form. It didn't. And then I sent the whole hot mess to Brenda Chin and she found the story and what was missing from Dylan and Jenny's journey to love. A few weeks later, and many long days at my desk, the book was back on track, and here it is! I hope you love it—we can all thank Brenda for saving this story from staying hidden on my hard drive forever.

A special thank you also goes to my Jeanster, Pamela Woodman Reeser, for suggesting "Fifty Shades" for Jenny's gray cat. I loved it! And soon Brant was finding this stray kitty "Fifty" in a box of romance novels. Get it?

Another thank you goes to my Jeansters reader group for encouraging me to put my dog Fish into a book. I finally did! I hope you enjoyed getting to know her a bit better.

A special thank you also goes to my error finding team. I appreciate your enthusiasm and joy—and eagle eyes. Thank you so much for being a part of my team.

* READER BONUSES *

BONUS 1:

Want to read Jenny and Dylan's wedding scene? (Fish pulls a Houdini act and tries to steal the show!) Put your email address in at www. jeanoram.com/SCbonus and enjoy these fun bonus scenes along with Jean's newsletter.

BONUS 2:

How about Karlene? What happened with Dylan's physical therapist and her Christmas wedding? Find out! When you sign up for Jean's newsletter you can download a complimentary copy of Karlene's runaway bride novella, A Tiny House Christmas. Read about her wedding day and the cowboy who comes to her rescue. Grab your copy at www.jeanoram.com/tinyhouse. Already getting my newsletters? Simply put in your email address—the one that receives Jean's newsletters and the novella is instantly yours!

GET A FREE BOOK & PLAY A GAME

* Didn't convince you to sign up for Jean's newsletter on the previous page with all of those delicious bonuses? Well, how about a free book? Get a complimentary ebook just for subscribing to Jean's newsletter. Get in touch with your inner bookworm and sign up today at www.jeanoram.com/freebook

* For readers who like games, be sure to check out "Find Fish" in the alternate, game version of the Sugar Cookie Country's House's original cover at www.jeanoram.com/Fish. See if you can find all nine of her in this fun version of the book's cover!

HOCKEY SWEETHEARTS

Have you read them all?

The Cupcake Cottage

Peach Blossom Hollow

Chocolate Cherry Cabin

The Peppermint Lodge

The Huckleberry Bookshop

Sugar Cookie Country House

The Gingerbread Cafe

A Tiny House Christmas

* * *

There are more stories set in Sweetheart Creek, Texas in these two series:

The Cowboys of Sweetheart Creek, Texas

The Cowboy's Stolen Heart (Levi)

The Cowboy's Secret Wish (Myles)

The Cowboy's Second Chance (Ryan)

The Cowboy's Sweet Elopement (Brant)

The Cowboy's Surprise Return (Cole)

MORE SMALL TOWN ROMANCES BY JEAN ORAM...

Veils and Vows

The Promise (Book 0: Devon & Olivia)

The Surprise Wedding (Book 1: Devon & Olivia)

A Pinch of Commitment (Book 2: Ethan & Lily)

The Wedding Plan (Book 3: Luke & Emma)

Accidentally Married (Book 4: Burke & Jill)

The Marriage Pledge (Book 5: Moe & Amy)

Mail Order Soulmate (Book 6: Zach & Catherine)

Blueberry Springs

Whiskey and Gumdrops (Mandy & Frankie)

Rum and Raindrops (Jen & Rob)

Eggnog and Candy Canes (Katie & Nash)

Sweet Treats (3 short stories—Mandy, Amber, & Nicola)

Vodka and Chocolate Drops (Amber & Scott)

Tequila and Candy Drops (Nicola & Todd)

Champagne and Lemon Drops (Beth & Oz)

The Summer Sisters

Falling for the Movie Star

Falling for the Boss

Falling for the Single Dad

Falling for the Bodyguard

Falling for the Firefighter

MORE SMALL TOWN ROMANCES BY JEAN ORAM...

Fairy Godmothers and Other Fiascos

Fairy Godmothers Aren't Cheap

Run, Run Rudolph

The Problem with Cupid

Indigo Bay

Sweet Matchmaker (Ginger and Logan)

Sweet Holiday Surprise (Cash & Alexa)

Sweet Forgiveness (Ashton & Zoe)

Sweet Troublemaker (Nick & Polly)

Sweet Joymaker (Maria & Clint)

ABOUT THE AUTHOR

Jean Oram is a *New York Times* and *USA Today* bestselling romance author. Inspiration for her small town series came from her own upbringing on the Canadian prairies. Although, so far, none of her characters have grown up in an old schoolhouse or worked on a bee farm. Jean still lives on the prairie with her husband, two kids, and big shaggy dog where she can be found out playing in the snow or hiking.

Become an Official Fan:
www.facebook.com/groups/jeanoramfans
Instagram: www.instagram.com/author_jeanoram
Facebook: www.facebook.com/JeanOramAuthor
Shop: shop.jeanoram.com
Newsletter: www.jeanoram.com/signup
Website & blog: www.jeanoram.com